UNDERBOSS

A WITH ME IN SEATTLE MAFIA NOVEL

KRISTEN PROBY

AMPERSAND PUBLISHING, INC.

Underboss

A With Me In Seattle MAFIA Novel

By

Kristen Proby

UNDERBOSS

A With Me In Seattle MAFIA Novel

Kristen Proby

Copyright © 2021 by Kristen Proby

Cover Design: By Hang Le

Cover photo: Wander Aguiar

Paperback ISBN: 978-1-63350-081-5

I *hate* these parties. Papa says I have to be here because it's a family duty, and I'm expected to be on my best behavior. Behave like a lady. Be alert, kind, passive.

I'm always alert.

I don't think I'm always kind, but I wouldn't say I'm mean, either. I mean, the other girls at the private school my parents send me to all seem to like me. I'm not like that mean girl, Shannon, who makes fun of the girls who haven't gotten their boobs yet.

I don't have boobs yet, either.

But I can't wait for the day I get them. Then maybe I won't hate coming to these stupid weddings the family is obligated to attend. They're so *boring*. But, someday, my boobs will grow, and the boys won't ignore me anymore.

No one will ignore me.

1

But back to my behavior. I'm not passive. And I'm not meek, even though I'm sure my father would prefer that I was. I talk too much. I ask too many questions. But I want to know everything there is to know about my family and the business we're in.

I take a sip of my Shirley Temple and scan the crowd. My parents are laughing with a bunch of other people—all old, like them. Papa puffs on a cigar. He doesn't usually smoke, but Mama doesn't mind if he does at events like this, in celebration.

The bride, in her white dress with its puffy sleeves, twirls around the dance floor with the groom, who doesn't look nearly as nervous as he did at the ceremony.

I thought he might pass out. He was green and shiny, and someone had to pass him a tissue to clean up the sweat on his forehead.

It was awesome.

I've seen most of these people before—usually at other weddings or funerals. I've heard Papa and Mama talk about the *families* and how it's important to maintain peace during these functions.

Whatever that means.

My big brother, Alex, is off chasing after some girl. I saw him looking her over with hungry eyes, giving her the kind of once-over he seems to do more often now that he's sixteen.

It's gross.

And when I told him so, he said I was just a baby and that I'd never understand.

But I'm not a baby. I'll be thirteen next month, after all. I'm practically a grown-up.

I blow out a breath, and when my eyes land on *him*, I feel my stomach clench. I haven't seen him before. He looks about Alex's age. Tall with dark hair and brown eyes. And he's laughing at something another boy said.

The guy looks as if he could be the dark-haired one's brother.

I smooth my hands down my red dress, square my shoulders, and walk over to him.

"Hi. I'm Nadia," I say and look all three of them in the eyes as I hold my chin high and wish I had bigger boobs. "I don't think I've met you before."

They turn quiet and look at me as if I'm a science experiment.

"Carmine," the most handsome one says. "And this is Shane and Rocco. My brothers."

"*Rocco?*" I snort. "Did your mother not like you very much?"

"It's a nickname," Rocco says with a shrug. "I like it better than Rafe."

"You're wrong." I prop a hand on my hip. "Rafe is much better. I want to talk to you."

I point at Carmine and then take his hand in mine, pulling him away from the others. We walk past the food table loaded down with shrimp and crab and then

3

move around a corner where we can have some privacy.

"Are you always this forward?" Carmine asks.

"Sure. What's the point in being anything else?"

His brown eyes narrow, and he looks me up and down. Once again, I'm reminded that I'm sorely lacking in the boob department.

I should have stuffed this stupid bra with something to make me look...*fuller.*

"What did you want to talk about?" he asks.

"I don't want to talk. I want to do this." Before he can reply, I boost myself up onto my toes and press my mouth to his. He squeaks in surprise, but he doesn't pull away.

I drop back onto my heels and stare up at him. Holy shit, for a first kiss, that was fun.

Really fun.

And he didn't even use any tongue.

"Look, Nadia—"

"Gotta go."

I turn and hurry away, suddenly embarrassed and not sure what to say. I just wanted to kiss him. To see what it was like.

And now, I know.

It was freaking awesome.

I smack into a hard chest. When I look up, my eyes meet my father's.

"What are you up to, little one?" he asks.

"Nothing." I shake my head. "I was just—"

"Do you know who that is?" he interrupts. Of course, he knows. He *always* knows. It's so annoying.

"Who?"

"That boy you were with."

I shrug a shoulder. "Carmine."

"Carmine *Martinelli*." I feel my eyes round. I've heard my father talk about that family before. "I want you to stay away from him. And his brothers. Is that understood?"

When his voice takes on that edge, I know he's not to be questioned. "Yes, sir."

"Good. Now, come on. They're cutting the cake."

I follow my father but glance back to find Carmine leaning his shoulder against the wall, watching me. A slow smile spreads over his face.

It's too bad he's off-limits.

CHAPTER 1

~CARMINE~

"*W*hen will you be back?"

I sip my whiskey and gaze out the window of the family's private jet, waiting for the pilot to get the go-ahead to take off.

"Depends on how this goes." I cross one foot over the opposite knee. "If it goes well, I don't know. If she tells me to go fuck myself, I'll be back tomorrow."

My younger brother, Shane, snickers on his side of the call. "From what I know of Nadia, she'll tell you to fuck off either way."

"True." I feel my lips twitch just as the pilot's voice comes over the speakers.

"We're cleared for takeoff, sir."

I push a button next to my seat. "Excellent."

"Have a safe trip," Shane says. "Keep me posted."

"Talk soon." I hit end on the screen and blow out a breath. No detail *hasn't* been scrutinized or picked apart. Nadia already knows me. There isn't anything I can do about that.

But she doesn't know what I have up my sleeve, and that's in my favor.

Now, I just have to get down to Miami—literally on the other side of the country from my home in Seattle—and make her fall in love with me.

I blow out a breath and tip my head back against the fine leather seat.

Piece of cake.

In opulence and luxury, the resort rivals any in any major city of the world. I've stayed in some impressive places, from Monte Carlo to the Maldives, and The Island Resort ranks right up there.

I'll be in the lap of luxury over the next few hours to days, and that doesn't disappoint.

I checked in, settled into my suite, and now I'm on the hunt for my prey.

I don't have to go far to find her.

I keep people on my payroll to give me the information I need the second I ask for it, and they've been on their toes when it comes to keeping track of the Bratva princess.

I walk through the resort spa to the private pool with its white chaise lounges, and sure enough, there she is, soaking up the sun in a pitiful excuse for a black bikini.

It's hardly more than two scraps of fabric, but it showcases Nadia's slim, tanned body to perfection.

At some point, she cut her blond hair into a short style that complements her stunning face nicely. I always forget how gorgeous she is until we're face to face, and it hits me like a punch to the gut.

"Is this seat taken?"

"No," she says without cracking open an eye. She looks serene. Relaxed. Almost as if she's about to fall asleep. She looks like the spoiled daughter of a powerful man.

Which is exactly what she is.

It's a comfortable eighty-two degrees outside as I lower myself onto the chair and stare at the Atlantic Ocean beyond the pool. I take a deep breath of salty air and turn to the woman next to me.

"It's a nice day, isn't it, Nadia?"

The use of her name has her slowly turning her head against the chair. She lowers her Chanel sunglasses down to the tip of her nose and takes me in from head to toe with those blue eyes.

"Carmine." My name sounds like acid on her tongue. "Fancy meeting you here."

"Funny coincidence, isn't it?" I grin and take the fresh glass of whiskey delivered by the waiter. "How's the family?"

Her eyes are cool as she sits up and sips the iced

drink at her elbow. The glass is sweaty as though it's been sitting for a long while, ignored. I can't help but watch her plump lips wrap around the straw.

With long, willowy limbs, full lips, ice-blue eyes, and light-colored hair, Nadia is a beautiful woman.

She's also a very dangerous one.

"Everyone is fine. Thank you for asking." She sets the glass aside. "And yours?"

"Oh, they're doing well. What brings you to Miami?"

"Vacation."

"Well, who can blame you? I'm here on a little holiday myself. It's still too cold in Seattle. I needed some sunshine."

"And you've found it."

I nod once, watching her. She looks relaxed. Calm. As if she doesn't have a care in the world. Then again, what could she possibly have to worry about?

Aside from me, anyway.

Because I'm about to chew her up and spit her out.

If I didn't hate her family so deeply, I might pity her.

"Do you have dinner plans?"

Her eyebrows climb in surprise. "Are you asking me out on a date, Carmine Martinelli?"

"A dinner among friends," I reply and shrug a shoulder as if it's the most natural thing in the world. "Our families are very old friends."

Two opposing mob families are hardly buddies.

"Right." She smiles now, and I can admit, my

stomach clenches in response. Yes, Nadia is breathtaking.

Fucking her won't be a hardship.

"I'm quite sure I can change my plans. What did you have in mind?"

"Something simple. Quiet so I can talk with you. Catch up. Meet me in the lobby at seven?"

"I'll be there."

I stand to leave, but before I can, her quiet voice calls me back.

"You look better than I remember," she says with a half-smile as her eyes travel down my torso to my swim-trunks-covered dick and back up again. "You grew up well."

"I could say the same for you." I nod and turn to leave, then toss over my shoulder, "Don't be late."

SHE STRIDES into the lobby at three minutes after seven, wearing a long, black gown with a dip in front that falls almost to her navel, displaying her cleavage. She's in shimmering silver shoes and carries a small clutch in her hand.

I don't doubt that she has a small pistol strapped to her inner thigh.

"You're late." I lean in to kiss her cheek.

"Am I?" She smiles coolly. "Well, I never was good at taking orders. I'm starved."

"Excellent. We're staying here for dinner."

I lead her into the hotel's steakhouse. The hostess shows us to our table, discreetly located in a quiet corner of the restaurant so we can be alone.

Once the wine has been poured and our appetizers and entrées ordered, Nadia sits back and studies me over the candles on the table set for two. She swirls the wine in her glass. Her mind is clearly whirling.

"What is it?" I ask her.

"How did you know I was here?" She doesn't miss a beat, and she's not coy.

Nadia is a clever woman.

I don't falter as I set my wine glass on the table. "I didn't. It was a happy coincidence."

"Bullshit."

I quirk a brow. "I'm a lot of things, Nadia, but I'm not a liar."

She sneers into her wine glass. "Right. The Martinellis are known for being upstanding citizens."

I laugh and then shrug as if to say: *What can you do?*

"I'm not here on behalf of the family. I'm here for some peace and quiet. And I ran into a beautiful woman that I happen to admire and find appealing. It's really that simple."

"Handsome *and* charming," she murmurs. "What a lovely surprise, indeed."

Dinner is lively. We talk about people we both

know. We flirt and laugh. And we both drink a little too much wine.

So much that two hours later, once we've consumed the food, and I've paid the hefty check, I don't bother asking her where her room is. I simply take her up to mine.

"Are you planning to seduce me, Carmine?"

"Yes." The answer is simple. And it might be the first truth I've spoken since I saw her at the pool.

"Excellent."

"WHERE ARE YOU GOING?" I catch Nadia's hand in mine and tug her onto my lap as she walks past me to the balcony.

"I need to make a call." Her voice is smooth as silk as she leans in and presses her lips to mine. She takes it further than just a peck, and just when I'm about to grab hold of her and tumble her onto the bed, she pulls away. Wearing nothing but the hotel robe, she saunters through the open glass door to the balcony beyond.

We moved from Miami to St. Petersburg last week. I rented a sexy little car, and we road-tripped across the state and up the west coast of Florida with the top down, enjoying each other's company and the views.

Now, we're checked into the Don Cesar resort, settled in another top-floor suite with magnificent views and top-notch service.

I watch Nadia pace the patio for several moments, her phone pressed to her ear, and then decide to get in a quick shower. We might actually leave the hotel today and do something besides each other.

I've spent the past two weeks with her, and I know our time together is running short. Aside from every inch of her delectable little body, I haven't learned anything about her family's secrets. She's a tight-lipped woman.

It's frustrating as fuck.

And, I can admit with reluctance, admirable.

I just finish washing my hair and turn off the water when she opens the bathroom door and grins when I step out of the glassed-in stall.

"Did your call go well?"

"Not exactly." The smile falls from her face, and her lips turn into a pout.

"What's wrong?"

"Nothing's *wrong,* exactly. I just won't be able to go home tomorrow as I originally planned. It looks like I need to book a room at the Ritz in Paris."

I dry my legs and wrap the towel around my hips. "Why Paris?"

"Paris is always a good idea, Carmine." She laughs and boosts herself up onto the countertop. "My house is being remodeled, and it won't be ready for at least six more months. So, I'll be living out of hotels for a while. And why not do that in my favorite city in the world? I'll shop and take in some culture."

"Come stay with me in Seattle."

The offer is past my lips before I even realize what in the hell I'm suggesting.

"That's ludicrous."

"Why?" I frame her face in my hands and brush my lips across hers. "Why is it ridiculous that I want to spend more time with you? Your home is unavailable, but mine is just sitting there."

"I've never really spent much time in your city," she says hesitantly as if she's actually considering it.

"I'd love to show you Seattle."

She sighs softly and rubs her nose over mine. "Are you sure about this? When your family finds out that you're practically living with a Tarenkov—"

"Let me deal with my family, darling. I'll make some calls right now so the condo is ready."

"You live in a condo?" She tips her head to the side.

"Yes, why?"

"You just strike me as a house man. A big, fancy one."

I have a fancy house, but you won't be living in it with me.

"Well, it's a big, fancy condo in the heart of downtown Seattle. Penthouse. So, I'm not exactly slumming it."

Her lips twitch.

"When would you like to go?" I ask as I bring up my assistant's contact on my phone. "Tonight?"

"Tomorrow," she says as she jumps off the counter and tugs my towel away. "I have plans for you today."

I pull the belt of her robe free and feel my dick harden at the sight of her small, firm breasts, already puckered and ready for my mouth. She lets the terrycloth drop to the floor, and when I simply reach out and plant my fingertip against her hard clit, she gasps.

Her body is responsive. And as much as I hate myself for it, I can't get enough of her.

I lift her and carry her back to the bedroom, where we tumble over already-mussed linens. She rolls on top of me, straddles my thighs, and tugs the skin of my neck between her teeth.

The bite stings, but only briefly before she licks me there, humming in delight.

I drag my fingertips up and down her calves. She's so fucking soft, so smooth. *Everywhere.*

"I'm going to ride you hard and fast," she mutters.

"No."

Her blue eyes meet mine in surprise.

"It's not going to be fast."

In one quick move, I have Nadia pinned under me.

"I'm going to take my time with you for the rest of the day. I'm going to make you moan, sigh, and forget your fucking name."

Her pupils dilate, and her breaths come faster with lust and anticipation.

I kiss my way down her torso and then nudge my

shoulders between her legs, spreading her wide. I feast until she's a writhing mass of lust, and my cock pulses with need.

I almost forget to reach for the condom but remember to sheath myself just before I plunge inside her. And then I still.

"Move," she insists, but I only grin down at her.

"Is this what you want?" Very slowly, I pull back, letting the rim of my dick glide against the walls of her womanhood. I'm not disappointed when she moans in delight.

"Faster."

"No."

I kiss her lips and slowly slide back in, torturing us both.

"You're not in charge right now, Nadia."

She whimpers, and I pull out again, then slam into her, making her gasp and open her eyes in surprise.

"Jesus, Carmine."

"No, darling. Just Carmine."

I take her on the ride of her life, moving effortlessly from slow and easy to fast and frenzied. Finally, when we're both sweaty and gasping, I let her fall over the edge into oblivion.

Enjoying Nadia has been a pleasure. Making her fall in love with me...seemingly effortless. If her last name weren't Tarenkov, I might let myself feel something for her other than simple desire.

But that's not the case. Because hatred has a pulse, and I have a job to do.

"WELL, you weren't kidding when you said it was fancy," Nadia says the next afternoon as we step off the private elevator into the penthouse. The truth is, the family owns the entire building. We use the apartments on the lower floors for many different things, such as offices and torture space. The penthouse is a luxury condo that we keep for guests—or for times like these when someone in the family needs to use it. "Look at this view!"

She hurries over to the heavy glass doors and opens them to the balcony. Puget Sound spreads out before us in all her glory, the blue water dotted with sailboats and ferries.

"You definitely can't beat the view."

I walk up behind her, rest my hands on the railing on either side of her, and kiss her smooth neck just below her golden hairline.

Nadia's short hair is sleek and sexy. Just as alluring as the long hair she's been known for.

"What made you decide to cut your hair?" I ask.

"I didn't." She turns in my arms and leans her elbows on the railing as she stares up at me. A slight breeze blows around us. "It was cut for me."

"By?"

She shrugs. "Doesn't matter."

I catch her face in my hand. "Who cut your hair, Nadia?"

She licks her lips. "I honestly don't know. I was ambushed. They cut it, broke a rib, and then disappeared. That's why I was in Miami. I needed to get away."

"Why hasn't your family tracked down who did that to you?"

As much as I hate the Tarenkovs, my blood boils at the thought of anyone laying a hand on this woman.

We don't hurt women. Ever.

"Because they don't know. I didn't tell them."

"Nadia—"

"Don't lecture me."

"Your father and brother need to know so they can protect you."

"*I* can protect myself."

"I don't doubt that for a moment. But someone was able to get to you. Why your hair?"

"I'm known for it. It's just hair, Carmine. It'll grow back. It was the broken rib that really pissed me off. Couldn't breathe right for a month. Now, let's drop it."

"For now. But we'll circle back to it. Now, would you like the grand tour of your new abode?"

"Hell, yes."

CHAPTER 2

~CARMINE~

Three Months Later...

"*I* love you." The lie rolls off my tongue easier than the first time I said it, just a few weeks ago. Nadia and I have become inseparable since she moved in with me. We fuck. We laugh. We eat.

And then we fuck some more.

I know her body better than I know mine. Every curve, every erotic inch that makes her writhe in ecstasy.

But it's a shot to my ego and my pride that I still don't know her mind. Nadia is good at keeping her thoughts close to her chest and only sharing bits and pieces of information. But she's loosened up considerably, and our time together has been fun.

So much so that I enjoy having her in my house.

No, not *mine*. I won't have the daughter of the man I hate most in the world living in my home. But she doesn't know that.

I press a kiss to her nape as she fusses with an earring, and then she smiles at me in the mirror.

"I love you, too, darling," she says. Her eyes go wide as I slip the diamond necklace around her neck from behind and fasten it with nimble fingers. "Oh my God, Carmine."

Her hand moves to touch the ice that glitters in the mirror.

"Later, when I make love to you, you'll wear this and nothing else."

Her gaze flies to mine, and she smiles quickly before turning to launch herself into my arms.

"You know I love gifts," she says against my mouth.

"And I love giving them to you." Nadia is spoiled. Selfish. Indulgent—all of the things I expected of her.

It's a pity that she didn't prove me wrong. Part of me wanted to respect her. To discover that she's nothing like the rest of her family.

But that didn't happen. Don't get me wrong, Nadia's been fun, but she's the typical, overindulged daughter of a powerful man; a woman used to getting her way.

She playfully tugs on my lower lip with her teeth, then walks across the room to open her Hermes bag, moving a few small things over to her tiny clutch.

"I hope nothing horrible happens today," she says

with a sigh. "It's Annika's wedding day. She deserves to have a happy day without any mafia shenanigans thrown in for good measure."

"Weddings, like funerals, are truce days. You know that." I fasten my cufflinks, the ones with the rubies that Nadia got me for my birthday last month. "Everyone will be on their best behavior."

We've been in Denver for three days, preparing for Nadia's cousin's wedding. Annika's groom, Richard Donaldson, has no ties to any mafia family, and that's the way Annika wanted it. Rumor has it that her family isn't thrilled, but they're permitting the union.

Reluctantly.

My family flew in yesterday. Nadia and I had dinner with my parents, Shane, Rocco, and my cousin, Elena, and her husband, Archer. Elena was raised like my sister. When someone murdered her parents, I took it upon myself to see to avenging their deaths.

Nadia's family *will* pay.

But not today.

Three other family organizations will also attend Annika and Rich's wedding. But there's an unwritten rule for weddings and funerals of mafia families. No violence. No retribution is to be dispensed on those days. They're days of celebration. Community. If beefs or scores need to be settled, it's for another time and place.

We may be brutal, but we *can* be respectful.

"My brother flies in this morning." Nadia checks

her lipstick in a handheld mirror, and I school my features.

Alexander Tarenkov will die at my hand. Not today, but one day soon. For his many transgressions.

"I was surprised he didn't come sooner."

"He was in Europe," she says with a shrug. "Doing what, I have no idea. You know he doesn't say much to me."

I smile as she takes one last look in the mirror. "Are you ready, sweetheart?"

"Ready."

"A TOAST," Igor Tarenkov says as he raises his glass and gets the attention of the roughly three hundred people at the reception. "To my niece, Annika. My little firefly. You make a lovely bride, my darling. And to Richard. If you fail to take care of my girl, you'll swim with the fishes. Cheers."

We laugh and raise our glasses as Igor sits at the table with his brother—Annika's dad—and Richard's parents, who look a little worse for wear.

"I don't think Rich's parents are used to people like us," I murmur to Nadia, who chuckles and sips her champagne.

"You'd be right. Annika said they're doctors from the suburbs."

"Just like her," I point out as the bride approaches our table.

"I'm so happy to see you," Annika says to Nadia as she leans in to kiss her cousin's cheek. "Are you all having a good time?"

"What's not to like?" Rocco asks.

"Hello, Rafe."

My brother's expression turns to a scowl. "I've told you a million times to call me Rocco."

"I will never do that," Annika replies with a straight face. "Your name is *Rafe*. That's what your mother calls you."

"You're not my mother," my brother reminds her.

"Isn't that fortunate?" Annika replies without missing a beat.

I always liked Annika. Like my cousin Elena, Annika has no interest in the family business. She's a doctor with a business in Denver. Her new husband, Rich, is also a physician.

They'll live a quiet life, making a good living from their jobs, even if Igor uses them from time to time to clean up a mess or two.

Having a doctor in the family is incredibly helpful.

Rocco narrows his eyes on Annika, but she just smiles at us. "Oh, I want you to meet someone. Ivie, come here."

I recognize the maid of honor as she hurries over to our table and offers us all a smile.

"Everyone, this is my best friend since we were six. Ivie Roberts."

"Hi." Ivie waves and flashes a shy smile. She's pretty but not beautiful. Not extraordinary like the other women in the room. "It's nice to meet you."

"The pleasure is all mine," Shane says as he takes her hand and kisses her knuckles. "You're lovely, aren't you?"

Rocco and I share a surprised look.

"Oh, it's just the dress," Ivie says, glancing down at the blood-red gown that fits her curvy body like a glove.

"No, I think it's the woman wearing it."

"How charming," Nadia says. "Ladies, let's make a trip to the champagne table."

Nadia loops her arms through Annika's and Ivie's and leads them away. Ivie glances back and gives Shane a sassy wink.

"Really?" I say to Shane, who just stares back at me blankly.

"What?"

"What do you mean *what*?" Rocco says with a laugh. "You were totally mooning over that girl. And she's not your type. She's not *any* of our types."

"What does that mean?" Elena demands, and Archer suddenly seems fascinated with the silverware on the table.

Smart man.

"She's fucking amazing," Shane replies with a scowl. "Did you *see* her?"

"Yeah." I nod slowly. "We saw her."

Without another word, Shane stands and goes in search of the woman, and Rocco lets out a laugh.

"What's wrong with her?" Elena demands again. "She's pretty."

"She's not ugly," I agree. "But she's hardly Shane's type. He goes for the cold, supermodel types."

"Like Nadia?" Elena asks with a cocked brow.

My eyes narrow on her. I don't know why I suddenly feel so defensive of the Bratva princess. I can't stand her.

"You don't understand." The words are clipped. Short.

But Elena doesn't back down.

"You know how I feel about this."

She thinks my mission's futile—is sure that Nadia doesn't have the answers, and that I'm wasting my time.

I think she's wrong.

"Let's dance," Nadia says, suddenly at my side. I take her hand, kiss the palm, and stand at her request.

"That would be a pleasure."

She leads me out to the dance floor. As the Goo Goo Dolls sing *Iris*, I pull Nadia to me, flush against me, and we move around the space.

Her lean body is a temptation that I never stop longing for. It'll be a pity that I won't get to fuck her anymore once all of this is said and done. I don't know that I've met a woman I've been so sexually compatible with before. I may not find one ever again.

The fire in her eyes as she gazes up at me tells me that she's just as fired up as I am.

Without another word, I take her hand and lead her off the floor, down a hallway, and to an empty storeroom that must be used as a maid's closet for the hotel.

I lock the door behind us and yank her against me.

"Did you do that on purpose?" I growl against her neck. "Seduce me on the dance floor so I'd be hard and wanting you?"

"Maybe." Her voice is breathy as her hands immediately reach for my slacks, pulling them open so she can plunge her hand inside to cup me. "Probably."

"Fucking hell." I turn and pin her against a shelving wall of folded sheets. I gather her skirt in my hands until it's up around her waist and then grin when I find her bare.

"I love it when you go without panties, babe."

"I know." She bites my earlobe. "Now, fuck me, Carmine."

She doesn't have to ask me twice. I retrieve the condom from my suit pocket, and when I plunge into her, I'm like a wild animal, unable to stop myself from fucking her hard and fast, punishing us both with the crazy rhythm I set.

"God, yes," she sobs and lets her head fall back against the sheets. "Fuck, yes."

It's over as quickly as it began. Once I dispose of the condom and we right ourselves, I open the door so we can return to the party.

Pandemonium hits.

"Oh, shit, what happened?" Nadia says as she hurries to the dance floor where a crowd has gathered. I follow.

We push our way to the front in time to see Armando, one of my father's men, seizing on the floor. He's foaming at the mouth, his face beet-red, eyes bulging.

"He's been poisoned," I mutter as I stare down at the man.

"I'll call the police," someone offers, but they're quickly taken aside.

We don't call the authorities.

And the fact that this was done *here*, with a mix of families and civilians, makes my blood boil.

I march over to Nadia's father's table, where my dad is already standing, his expression mutinous.

"That drink was meant for *me*," Pop says. "Armondo grabbed it by accident. We laughed about it, and then I flagged down the waiter for another. Moments after drinking it, that"—he gestures to the floor —"happened."

"Are you implying that I ordered your murder at my niece's wedding?" Igor asks, his tone mild. "I'm not the only boss here, Carlo."

"Yours is the only family the Martinellis have an issue with," Pop replies.

Shane and Rocco stand beside me, all of us behind our father. Nadia and her brother, Alexander, stand behind their father.

My gaze holds Nadia's.

"I don't know what you're talking about," Igor says. "I've never done anything to you or your family."

"You had my sister killed," Pop immediately replies.

"I always liked Claudia," Igor says and drums his fingers on the table. "Vinnie, not so much. He was a pitiful excuse for a man and certainly had no business being the boss of your organization. But I suppose that's none of my business."

"So you killed him," Pop says.

"I certainly did not," Igor says and leans forward. "No one in my organization is responsible for Vinnie's or Claudia's deaths. If I was, I would take responsibility for it."

My father nearly vibrates with his fury.

"What good would that do me?" Igor continues. "The Bratva is successful, thriving, without the need for war. Just because I thought Vinnie was a worthless piece of shit doesn't mean I ordered his death. And I certainly wouldn't give the order to have you, my *friend*, Carlo, killed at my firefly's wedding."

"Then what the fuck is going on?" I demand and scan the crowd. Someone took Armondo's body away and cleaned up the floor. The guests murmur quietly. The DJ started the music again.

Only at a mafia wedding could someone get murdered and have the party carry on as if nothing at all happened.

"Clearly, someone has it out for our families," Igor says. "Nadia."

Nadia places her hand on her father's shoulder. "Yes, Papa?"

"I'm assigning this to you."

"Carmine will help you," Pop agrees, and I feel my back straighten.

"I don't need to involve Nadia in this."

"I've just involved her," Igor says. "You've been playing house for weeks, and nothing has come of it so far. Let's change tactics."

My eyes move to Nadia's, and right before me, the warmth I've seen in those blue orbs freezes.

"Did you honestly think I was in love with you?" She smirks. "Grow up, Carmine."

I should have seen it. I should have known that she was double-crossing me. Maybe I did. Perhaps I ignored it.

I'm a fucking idiot.

"It's decided," Pop says. "You two will hunt down those responsible for what's happened here today. And for my sister's death."

With the wave of a hand, we're dismissed. Before Nadia can run away, I corner her and turn her to me.

"What?" She glares up at me.

"What was the end game?" I ask, my voice hard as stone.

"I didn't have one. Yet." Her gaze falls to where my hand rests on her arm. "I didn't give you permission to touch me."

I feel the smile slowly spread over my lips. "So, it's true what they say? You're nothing but an ice princess."

She doesn't even flinch. "And you'd do well to remember that. I don't want your help with this."

"You have it anyway."

"I said—"

"Do you think I give two fucks what you said?" I lean in to her. "We work together. Starting now. No more show. No more lies."

"No more sex."

I chuckle. "Darling, you couldn't keep your hands off me if you tried."

"Watch me."

CHAPTER 3

~NADIA~

"What are you doing here?" Papa asks as I walk into his Denver office. He frowns and sets a pen on the notebook he was scribbling notes in. "You're supposed to be in Seattle with Carmine."

"I'm not going to Washington." I pace to the window and stare down at Coors Field, downtown Denver, and the mountains beyond. I have to admit, it's a beautiful city. Once you get past the high altitude, it's one of my favorite places. But I'm not here to admire the scenery.

"Carmine is in Seattle," Papa reminds me.

"I believe so."

"So, I'll ask again, what are you doing here?"

"I don't need to be with Carmine," I say and watch as a crane works on a skyscraper. "I can work just fine without him. Better, actually."

"You're supposed to be working together."

"Now that the charade is over, there's no need."

"That's not your decision to make."

His stern voice has me turning to look at him.

"We don't trust each other." I cross to my father. "For good reason. The Martinellis think we had their family members killed."

"We didn't."

"You and I know that, but convincing them is another matter entirely. And why would he work with me anyway?"

"Because he's been ordered to do so."

I roll my eyes and then sigh as I sit in the chair opposite my father.

"You've worked hard for your entire adult life to be taken seriously in this family," Papa says thoughtfully. "You don't question orders. Why now?"

"Alex wouldn't want to work with him, either."

"Did you fall in love with him?"

I scowl at the absurdity of the suggestion. "Absolutely not. He's a liar—and not a particularly good one. And he's a Martinelli."

"He's also young and handsome."

And excellent in bed, but I'm sure my father doesn't want to know that.

"I'm not young and stupid," I remind him. "I just didn't see the value in following him to Seattle when what we're looking for most likely isn't there."

"It's a place to start," he replies and waves me off.

"Get up there. *Today*, little one. And keep me apprised of the situation."

"Yes, sir."

I stand and turn to leave.

"Nadia?"

"Yes?" I spin back to him.

"I love you."

I smile and blow him a kiss. "I love you, too, Papa."

THERE'S a car in his circular driveway. I don't think the older Cadillac belongs to Carmine.

I park behind it just as the front door opens, and Carmine steps out with another man. The unknown person nods and then gets into his vehicle and drives away.

I slam the door of my rented Lexus and send Carmine a sassy grin as I climb the steps of his house.

"I knew you were the big, fancy house type."

"How did you find out where I live?" he asks by way of greeting.

"Oh, Carmine." I pat his cheek and breeze right past him and inside, not bothering to wait for an invitation. "Don't insult either of us by asking stupid questions. You knew plenty about me before you found me in Miami. And I know more about you than you'd probably be comfortable with."

"I just have one question," he says as he follows me

into his living room. "Is your house really being remodeled?"

I cross to the mantel and run the pad of my finger over a little owl statue there. "I don't have a house. If you'd done more research, you'd know that."

"Maybe you live in a house owned by your father," he suggests.

"I bounce from place to place," I say without elaborating. I walk over to a painting and touch the name of the artist. "You have a lot of expensive knickknacks."

"Are you going to simply walk through my house and touch everything?" I notice his teeth are clenched, his hands fisted. It fills my heart with glee.

Pissing him off is a pleasure.

"Maybe." I smirk and wander into the kitchen. "I'm starved. I couldn't stomach the crap they served on the plane. I know you have a private jet, but I went ahead and jumped on a commercial flight this morning. Even first class turned my stomach."

I open his fridge and take inventory of the contents. I pull out a cheese and cracker tray and dig in.

"This salami is fantastic. Where did you find it?"

"You'd have to ask the caterer." He leans his hip against the island and crosses his arms over his impressive chest.

Carmine Martinelli is the male version of beautiful. He looks like a fallen angel. With that thick, dark hair, those deep brown eyes, and full lips that could turn a girl inside out, he's an impressive specimen.

No, I didn't fall in love with him.

But I enjoyed him. Every chance I got.

"You look well," I say and pop a cracker into my mouth. "But you have some bags under your eyes. Not sleeping well?"

There are no bags. He looks fucking magnificent. But seeing the spark of annoyance flicker in his eyes is worth the dig.

"What do you want, Nadia?"

"We're working together, remember?" I shrug a shoulder and open a jar of green olives. I didn't lie about being hungry. I'm suddenly starving.

"Given that I haven't heard a peep from you since the wedding, I figured you'd blown that off."

"A peep?" I snicker and chew on another olive. "You're cute, Carmine."

He huffs out a breath of annoyance.

I love ruffling his feathers.

"Anyway, I thought I'd come to Seattle and see you. Find out what you know."

"I'm working on some leads."

I nod slowly. "What kind of leads?"

"Rumors. Making calls."

"The mafia is good at keeping secrets, aren't they?" I shake my head and close the food containers back up, then return it all to the fridge. "Bastards put a lot of bullshit in this world, but when it comes to covering their tracks, they're damn good at it."

"What do *you* know?" he asks.

"I did get a call when I got off the plane," I admit and walk over to him. I brush my finger down the buttons of his white shirt. "I always did like looking at you in these white button-downs."

He catches my hand in his and pushes me away.

"What did the caller say?"

The rebuff hurts my feelings more than expected—and more than it should. But I keep my face schooled in the sneer I've worn since I arrived.

"A new chemical's being passed around," I say casually. "It's lethal. Highly addictive. And in large quantities, can cause seizures and foaming at the mouth."

"Who—?"

"I'm not going to tell you that," I say smoothly. "And you know it. That's all I know for now. I really should go. I'll be in touch."

I march away from him before I do something monumentally stupid, like strip him naked and suck his cock.

Carmine has a grade-A penis.

And it's off-limits.

"Have a good day."

"Wait," he says as he hurries after me. "Where are you staying?"

"Oh, don't worry. I'll be around."

"Nadia."

"Goodbye, Carmine."

I hop in the car and zoom away from his house.

I'm not good at emotions. I'm excellent at keeping

myself aloof. Cold, even. I don't mind being called the ice princess at all. Because when emotions get tangled up in business, you die.

And I'm not ready to meet Satan yet. Or, should I say, he's not ready for me?

I don't like that I feel things when I'm around Carmine. It's purely physical.

"Yeah, keep telling yourself that," I mutter as I drive toward the freeway.

I knew the several months I spent with Carmine were a lie. He didn't love me, and I certainly didn't love him. We were merely playing house. Manipulating each other.

But we also had fun. We laughed a lot. We got along well. And the sex...

Well, let's not go there.

I enjoy him. And that's the part that annoys the hell out of me. Because he's a Martinelli, and my father told me when I was thirteen that anyone with that name was off-limits.

Nothing has changed in that regard.

So, I'll do as my father asked and keep an eye on Carmine, but I'll also keep my distance.

For my fucking sanity.

Because I'm going to be the next boss. My brother doesn't have the chops—he's too selfish, too immature.

I can't stand him.

I'm the one who studied at my father's knee since I

was a child. I'm the one who pays attention and does as she's told.

And I'm often overlooked because I'm a woman.

But that won't stop me.

I'll do my job here and continue proving to my father that *I'm* the one who should step up after he's gone.

THE HOTEL just wasn't cutting it. Too many people were in and out. Too many eyes. I know that Carmine has eyes on me, but I was making it too easy on him.

So, I checked out two days ago and secured a vacation rental by owner, a VRBO, instead. I used my father's assistant to make the reservation, so my name's nowhere on the application.

I like being anonymous. Carmine wasn't wrong. My family owns the condo I live in just outside of Atlanta, and my name isn't on that one either. I don't want anyone to trace me back to any holdings. I want to be mysterious.

It's hard for the bad guys to find you if they can't figure out where you live.

Not that they didn't find me anyway, I muse, rubbing a hand over the rib that still sometimes gives me fits.

I haven't heard anything on the drug thing for days. I'm basically just sitting in Seattle, twiddling my thumbs. I could do this from *anywhere.*

But Papa wants me here.

I blow out a breath and shut my laptop. I've been calling in favors and making calls, and I'm going nowhere fast. It's like I'm two inches away from getting the information I need, but then it gets tugged just out of my reach.

It doesn't help that I don't know exactly what I'm looking *for*. The simple news of a new drug doesn't give me much to go on. That happens every day in every city, and my family isn't into the drug-dealing scene.

Maybe our fathers have us on a wild goose chase, just to see if they can pull the strings and have us follow along like good little puppets.

I wouldn't put it past them.

I need some air, so I slide my feet into my running shoes, grab my windbreaker, and set off on a jog.

This little neighborhood near the water is beautiful. Full of older homes, it's clearly an established neighborhood with low crime and little drama.

I would generally think of it as boring.

My pace is steady as I climb the first hill. Seattle is nothing if not hilly, but it makes for a good workout so I'm not complaining.

I just hit my stride when something sails over my head, and someone lifts me from behind.

"Let go of me, you asshole!" I'm kicking and flailing about, but it's no use. I can't see who grabbed me.

So I go limp. Deadweight.

The man holding me grunts with the effort it takes to hold me, but throws me onto a seat of a vehicle. And then we're moving.

"Who the fuck are you?" I demand.

No one replies.

I know there are at least two of them. The one who grabbed me and the other who's driving.

Fuck, this isn't good.

They could kill me and dump me. My father would rain hell down on them, but they could still do it.

The vehicle—van?—parks, and I'm jerked out and taken down what feels like a series of hallways. Finally, they dump me onto a chair and tie my hands behind my back.

"What the fuck?" I ask—and am punched in the jaw.

I see stars. My mouth throbs.

"You're asking a lot of questions."

I frantically search my brain to place the voice. Have I heard it before? It doesn't sound familiar.

"And that pisses you off," I guess.

Someone punches me again, in the left eye this time.

"We're going to teach you to keep your questions to yourself, bitch."

The beating is ruthless. By the time they dump me on some random sidewalk in downtown Seattle, I'm bloody, bruised, and quite sure my right shoulder is dislocated.

It's hard to breathe.

I pull the bag off my head but can't see out of my left eye. What I can see is clouded and red because of the blood in my right eye.

Christ, I don't know what to do.

I can't go to the hospital. And I'm never stepping foot in that VRBO again.

How did they find me?

I'm going to pass out, and I don't want to do that here, so I stumble to my feet and look around. I'm in an industrial area. People walk about, but they don't look my way.

It's as if women are dumped, bloody and broken, every fucking day.

Whoever grabbed me didn't take my phone, so I pull it out of the sleeve in my leggings and punch in the address for the condo that Carmine and I lived in for several months. I know his family owns the building, and no one lives in the penthouse full time.

I'll crash there until I figure out what to do.

According to my cell, I'm only a couple of blocks away. I hobble toward the building, having to stop and lean on the concrete to catch my breath a few times.

Did they break another goddamn rib?

It takes five times longer than it should to reach Carmine's building. I'm ecstatic to discover that my codes still work on the door and the private elevator that leads up to the penthouse.

When the apartment doors open, I step in and lean against the wall as I listen for any movement inside.

There's nothing.

It doesn't appear as if anyone's been here since Carmine and I were here before leaving for Denver last week.

Has it really only been a week?

The red roses Carmine got me are still on the sofa table, wilting. A pair of my heels lay on the floor next to the kitchen island.

This is the only safe place for me in the city. I need to call my father, but that will have to come later. I'm not even sure what my name is right now.

The adrenaline of the attack is wearing off, and I know I'm going to be sick. Nausea roils my stomach, and dizziness fills my head. I just want to *sleep.* I probably shouldn't. I most likely have a concussion, but I'll be fine.

Everything will be fine.

God, I hurt. More than I ever have in my life.

I swing by the kitchen to grab a bucket from under the sink in case I do throw up, and then stumble to the couch in the living room. The sofa is huge, deep, and so comfortable that Carmine and I took many an afternoon nap here, tangled up with each other.

We also fucked like rabbits on it, but I'll think about that later.

The moment I lie down, I feel exhaustion overtake me. But the rest is fitful—I can't get comfortable. I can't catch my breath.

I really should call an ambulance. My father would

not be pleased, but I'm alone, and something is very wrong.

I feel the anxiety building in my stomach. I reach for my phone, only to discover that I set it on the counter in the kitchen.

I want to cry.

Everything screams in agony.

And, suddenly, someone looms over me.

CHAPTER 4

I'm in the middle of my second set of pull-ups when my phone rings.

I ignore it.

I've been pissed for days. Does Nadia think she can just waltz into my home, taunt me, and then breeze out again? That she can smirk at me and act as if I haven't had her in every position imaginable? That I don't affect her at all?

I won't admit to anyone that she got under my skin.

But goddamn it, she did.

My phone rings again. When I drop to the floor, I accept the call.

"What?"

"I'm sorry to interrupt you, sir. You need to come to the penthouse."

I narrow my eyes. "What happened?"

"Nadia's here, sir. And she's going to need you."

"I'll be there in thirty."

I end the call and, without another thought, hurry to grab my keys and wallet, then get into my car and peel out of the driveway, headed toward the freeway.

I like living away from the areas where we conduct business. I like keeping things separate. My grandmother taught me the importance of that.

But in times like these, it's a royal pain in the ass.

Thanks to traffic on the freeway, I make it to the building in twenty-six minutes, park in my reserved space, and take the private elevator up to the penthouse.

What in the hell is Nadia doing back here? Gathering the things she left behind when we went to Denver? That made sense.

But when I step off the elevator, I instinctively know that something is very wrong.

The space is still. The blinds are still closed, so it's mostly dark inside.

I flip on a hallway light to illuminate the area and see Nadia's blond head on the couch.

She's lying down.

And when I approach her, every drop of blood in my veins boils.

"Don't hurt me," she moans. "Can't."

"Nadia." I squat next to her and take in her bruised and bloodied face. "It's Carmine. I'm not going to hurt you."

"Carmine?" She lets out a small gasp through cut and bloody lips. "Didn't know where to go."

"You came to the right place. No one will think to search for you here. I have to call my people to come in and take care of you."

"No."

"Yes." I kiss her bloody hand. "I'll take care of this."

I pull out my phone and call our medical team. After they assure me that they're only minutes away, I hang up and hurry into the bathroom where I wet a washcloth and return to start cleaning her face as best I can so I can see the extent of her injuries.

"Hurts."

"I know." My voice is clipped, even to my ears. It takes everything in me to be gentle.

All I want to do is get my hands on the piece of shit who did this and make them pay. Painfully. Slowly.

Horrifically.

The elevator slides open, and the three men we employ to handle our medical needs come marching in.

"Christ," Malloy says with a hiss. "What did you do to her?"

"If you want to keep your job, you'll never ask that again," I bark as I step back and let them take over. At first, Nadia recoils from their touch, but with some soothing murmurs, she finally relaxes and lets the men examine her.

"I can't tell if her vision's been affected in this eye,"

Malloy says grimly. "It's swollen shut. I'll need to take another look in a few days."

He stands and pulls me aside as the other two continue working their magic with gauze and antiseptic.

"I've never suggested this before, and I know it's not how we do things…" Malloy begins and then props his hands on his hips. "But she needs to be in the hospital, Carmine."

I shake my head, but Malloy continues.

"She's been beaten so severely; I don't know if she has internal bleeding or a punctured lung. Her shoulder may be dislocated, and we might have to reset it. I recommend leaving the room for that one."

"I won't go."

He swallows and shakes his head. "Whoever did this was obviously given an order to fuck her up and leave her just this side of dead. And that's what they did. I have no idea how she even got herself up here."

"Because she's stubborn and damn smart. I'm not taking her to the hospital."

"Sir—"

"No. We'll take care of her here. Do your damn job, Malloy."

His mouth flattens into a line, and then he nods once. "I'm going to give you a list of things to watch for. If even *one* of them shows up, you need to call an ambulance right away. I mean it."

It's brutal standing back and watching them care

for her. I feel helpless. She screams when they move her shoulder, but it's not dislocated—just wrenched badly. She whimpers when they poke and prod to see if anything is broken.

They hook her up to an IV and start pumping her full of antibiotics and morphine to help with the pain. Before long, she's settled back on the big couch with fresh dressings, a blanket, and orders to stay and rest for at least a week.

I'll personally see to it that she fucking obeys that order.

After my men leave, I return to her and gently brush her hair off her face.

"Sorry," she murmurs drunkenly.

"For what?"

"You're mad."

I sigh and lean over to press my lips to her forehead. "Not at you. When I find out who did this, I'll kill them."

"Get in line."

"Do you know who it was?"

She licks her swollen lips. "No. Couldn't see. Water?"

"Of course."

I hurry to the kitchen and fill a glass with crushed ice, and then bring it back to her.

"Here, suck on this."

"Mm." She sucks greedily on a chunk. "Nice."

"I'll be right here, Nadia. I'm not going anywhere.

You sleep now and get healed up so you can kick some ass."

"Yeah." She sighs but reaches for my hand. "Stay."

"I told you, I'm here. I promise, I won't go."

"'Kay."

She slips into sleep, and I pull my hand down my face.

What the fuck? An hour ago, I wanted to spank her ass. Now, I want to protect her, fight for her. Keep her safe.

Because the truth is, she *has* gotten under my skin. That doesn't mean I trust her, but she didn't deserve this.

"KING ME."

Nadia scowls down at the checkerboard. "You're cheating."

"Negative." I stand and walk into the kitchen to get more chips.

We've been in the penthouse for five days. She slept the first three away, allowing her body to heal.

And now she's up and showered, her arm in a sling, scowling at me over a checkerboard.

"Is there any queso left?"

"No, you ate it all last night. At least your appetite is back."

"Yeah, well, I like food. You know that."

I grin, thinking back on all of the fun meals we'd had together. "I do. Watching you eat isn't a hardship. Where have you been staying? I'll have someone go and gather your things. Bring them here."

"I can go get my stuff soon enough."

"Why won't you tell me?"

"You probably already know."

I do. But she doesn't need to know that.

"Nadia, I think we're in the truce zone here. Think of this like a wedding or a funeral."

"Yeah, well, it almost *was* my funeral. And I don't know that it wasn't *you* who ordered this to be done to me," she blurts and stands to walk to the window. "You got here awfully fast after it happened."

I have to shove my hands into my pockets. Just six months ago, I would have said that nothing this woman could say or do could hurt me.

But things have changed.

And it seems she *can* hurt me.

That's unsettling and something to think about later.

She turns at my silence. The bruises on her face are beginning to fade from black to a sickly purple.

"You won't deny it?" she demands.

"I don't know how your family does things," I begin slowly, "but in *my* family, I've been taught to *never* hurt women. Physical punishment is not tolerated when it comes to women. Ever, under any circumstances."

I remember the day my cousin Elena first showed

51

me the scars on her body she'd sustained at the hands of her father, my uncle. More anger seethes through me.

"Maybe not everyone in your family feels that way."

"They do." Agitated, I pace the floor. "I can say, without a shadow of a doubt, that my family is not responsible for this."

"Maybe one of your brothers—"

"IT WASN'T US!" I shout at her and then swear under my breath. "For fuck's sake, Nadia, no. I may not know what to feel when I'm around you, but I know that I wouldn't hurt you. No one in my family would hurt you. *You* haven't done anything to my family or me."

"Except make you think I'd fallen in love with you. Fucked your brains out. Moved in with you."

"Good sex isn't worth maiming over."

She shakes her head.

"I'm not convinced that your family isn't responsible for my aunt's and uncle's murders. And if they are, they *will* pay. I guarantee you that."

"If my father gave that order, he would cop to it," she says with a sigh. "I admit, I don't know every single order he's given, but he's not one to kill and then deny or deflect. He takes ownership of his decisions without regret. If he was behind those murders, he'd say so."

I can tell she believes what she's telling me.

"But, at the end of the day, we don't trust each other," she continues.

"Do you remember what happened when I found you here?"

"You were *so* pissed at me," she says.

"No." I cross to her, needing to touch her. "I told you then, and I meant it. I wasn't angry with you. I was livid that someone—*any*one—had put their hands on you this way. The fury was, and still is, a breathing thing inside me. I would have been upset to see any woman hurt like this, but the fact that it was *you* made it so much worse. So, no, we may not fully trust each other, but damn it, I care about what happens to you. I don't want to see *anything* happen to you. And we've been given orders to work *together*. To figure this mess out and get it resolved. I don't know what's happening now, with the murder at the wedding and your attack. I don't know if it has anything to do with my aunt and uncle, but I need to find out. I have connections that you don't and vice versa. We're stronger in this together. So, until we resolve this, you're stuck with me."

Her blue eyes slide to mine. "What do you mean?"

"You'll be staying with *me*. I can't protect you the way we've been doing things, obviously."

"I don't need—"

"Just stop talking." In exasperation, I march away from her. "Yes, you're strong and badass, and you can take care of yourself. But right now, people want to hurt you, and I'm partly responsible for that. There's a team of people here to help keep us safe. And goddamn it, that's what you're going to let me do."

"So, I'm being held hostage?"

I grunt but can't help but start laughing. "Yes. Clearly, this luxury penthouse is a horrible situation. I feel for you, Nadia. But keep a stiff upper lip. Suck it up and deal with it."

She snorts. "No sex. I mean it."

"I'm not in the habit of forcing unwilling women to fuck me."

Her face sobers at the steel in my voice. "I didn't mean to insinuate that you'd rape me."

"I need some fresh air."

She nods and glances at her phone when it rings.

"Not gonna answer?"

"I have no intention of speaking to my father. At least for a few more days."

I narrow my eyes. "Why haven't you told him about this?"

"Because. And the reasons are none of your business."

"If you confide in him, you could live wherever the fuck you want. He'd send protection, *and* he'd start his own hunt for the bastards who touched you. Nadia—"

"You have the luxury of trusting your family," she interrupts. "It's not something we share."

I step back, surprised. "You don't trust your family? When it comes to the business we're in, trusting them is of the utmost importance."

"My father, yes. I know he loves me and would do anything to protect me." She swallows hard. "But I don't trust my brother at all."

That's something we can agree on. Alexander Tarenkov is a slimy piece of shit, and it would make my black heart happy to tear him limb from limb with my bare hands.

"Why?"

"Alex is a selfish man," she says simply. "Only concerned with himself and how to manipulate every situation to his advantage. He'd make a horrible boss. The family, the *organization*, would collapse within a year. I don't know what shady deals he has going on the down-low, but I'd guess there are a few of them. No. I shouldn't be telling you any of this."

With a sigh, she lowers herself to the couch.

"I hate your brother with every fiber of my being." My voice is flat as I sit across from her. "There's nothing honorable about him."

"I know."

"Do you think he's behind everything that's going on?"

"No." She smirks. "He's a pussy. He doesn't have the balls to kill anyone. Alex is self-serving, yes, but he's also content to ride just under the radar. I do think he's laundering money that he's hiding from Papa. And when he's found out? Well, let's just say it won't go over well.

"But killing another family's boss? Possibly starting a war? No. He's not smart enough for that."

Unfortunately, I agree with her. He's slimy to the core but also as weak as they come.

And not especially intelligent.

"So, in the meantime, you've been attacked twice, and your father has no idea."

"He'll be angry," she admits. "But until I figure out who's behind it and everything else, I'll keep it to myself. Besides, what's done is done. He can't undo it."

"If I kept something like this from my father, he'd be *livid*."

"You're lucky," she says. "That your family is so close. That it's your safe haven."

"You need that, too. Our business is too lonely to be alone, Nadia."

"I'm not alone. I'm being held hostage, remember? So, what now? What's our next move?"

"We're staying here for another week."

She scowls, but I hold up my hand to stop her from saying anything more.

"You're healing, but you're still fragile. When we get out of here, I need to make sure that you're well and capable of having my back. We're likely going to get into a couple of sticky situations. As long as you're feeling up to it, we'll go to New York next week."

"Have you called the Sergis?"

"I'll call Billy when I have a solid date." No mob family travels to another family's territory without alerting them and asking for permission. It's a code we all live by and respect.

So, the fact that someone was in Seattle to hurt Nadia only intensifies my anger.

No one should have been here.

"They hate me there."

"*Hate* is a strong word," I remind her.

"And accurate."

"You'll be with me."

"What if they hate you, too?"

I smile thinly. "They don't."

CHAPTER 5

~NADIA~

"I'm bored out of my *mind*." I pace the penthouse in front of the windows. "It's been two damn weeks. I feel great. I can even cover what's left of the bruises with makeup, and you'd never know they're there."

Carmine lounges on the couch, reading something on his iPad.

"What are you doing?"

"Reading stock reports." He sips his coffee. "How are your investments doing?"

I cock my head to the side. "Are you some kind of financial advisor?"

His grin is wide and toothy—and cockier than any one man has a right to be.

"I have a master's in finance," he says. "I guess you could say that I'm a financial advisor."

"To your family," I finish for him. "You help them hide money."

There's that smile again. "I assure you, everything I offer is legal."

"Bullshit."

"So, I'll ask again. How are your investments?"

He's evading.

"I don't have any."

His brow knits. *"None?"*

"No."

"Nadia, you're pushing thirty. You should have a Roth IRA, at the very least. You should have stocks. I know you're set to inherit more money than the net worth of several countries, but—"

"Carmine. I don't want to talk about finances. I want to get the hell out of here."

He sighs. "Let's go for a walk."

"Anything." I bounce into the bedroom to snatch up the new shoes I ordered a few days ago. Since blood now covered the running shoes I had on the day I was attacked, I needed new ones.

When I'm dressed and ready to go, Carmine sets his iPad aside, and we step into the elevator.

"We should head to New York tomorrow," I say as we ride down to the ground floor.

"It's Friday, Nadia. Let's go Monday."

"Because the mafia takes weekends off?" I roll my eyes. "You're stalling."

"I told you before; I want to make sure you're healthy."

"I feel great." It's not a complete lie. Aside from a little ache in my shoulder when I raise my arm above my head, and the vision in my left eye still being a little blurry, I feel pretty good. The doctor said I might not get my sight back all the way, though.

That pissed me right off.

But I'm not dead, and that's something.

"I saw you wince this morning when you reached for a mug in the cabinet."

"You're watching me like a fucking mother hen." I scowl as we step outside and then stop to take a deep breath. "I love summer."

"Seattle is nice in the summer," he says. "Less rain, more sun. Not too hot, thanks to the Sound."

"It's a beautiful day." I tip my head up to the sky.

"You might want to pay attention, so you don't face-plant on the concrete."

I laugh and glance up at him. "You would probably catch me."

"Maybe."

These past two weeks have shown me that I can let my guard down around Carmine. Now that it's just *us* —no pretenses, no blatant lies or games—I actually trust that he won't hurt me.

Not intentionally, anyway.

He's the only person in the world that I *can* trust

right now, and I just hope that he doesn't do something stupid to betray that faith.

"What's that place?" I ask, pointing across the street. "It looks like a coffee shop. Cherry Street Coffee House. How did I not know that was here all the time we've lived here?"

"I don't think I've been in there," he says. "Do you want some coffee?"

"Yes. An iced Americano sounds awesome right now. Let's do it."

We watch for traffic and then hustle across the street. The café is so cute, and it smells *amazing* when we walk inside.

I order my iced coffee and throw caution to the wind, including an orange and cranberry scone. Carmine gets the same. Before long, we're walking out of the shop again, loaded down with our treats.

"This is the best day I've had in two weeks."

Carmine laughs. "If I'd known that all it took for you to have the best day ever is a coffee and a scone, I would have done this sooner."

"Now we know. This could be a new daily occurrence."

"I overheard the barista telling someone that they have killer cinnamon rolls." Carmine shrugs as he takes a bite of his scone. "Maybe we'll have to check it out for breakfast."

"God, yes." I sip my coffee in happiness. "It feels good to finally feel semi-normal, you know?"

"I imagine that it does," he replies. "And it's good to see you looking like yourself again."

"I think that—*whoa!*"

My toe catches on an uneven part of the sidewalk, and I pitch forward. My coffee flies, and before my face can hit the ground, Carmine's arm wraps around my waist, and he catches me.

It all happened so fast, yet at the same time, it seemed to be in slow motion.

Especially the part where my almost-full coffee fell and splashed *everywhere.*

"Sonofabitch," I growl. "I was enjoying that."

"You can have mine." Carmine makes sure I'm standing upright and offers me his cup, but I shake my head.

"No, you enjoy it. I still have my scone."

"We'll share," he says, and then his eyes narrow on my face. "What hurts?"

I don't want to tell him. I don't want to say it out loud because then it'll be true.

"I'm fine."

His finger gently taps under my chin, and he makes me look him in the eyes.

"Don't fucking lie to me, Nadia."

"My shoulder." I sigh in exasperation. "I wrenched it a bit when my arm flailed. But it'll be fine. I'll just ice it and take an Advil when we get back. It'll be just fine."

He sighs and offers me a sip of his coffee, which I accept.

"Let's head back."

I'm tired. I didn't expect our walk to exhaust me as much as it did. Maybe it was the almost-fall that did me in.

The return trip is more subdued. We're quiet as we sip Carmine's coffee and eat our scones. When we get up to the penthouse, Carmine orders me to sit on the sofa.

"I'm getting you some ice," he informs me. His tone says he's not to be argued with.

I'm not really interested in arguing anyway.

The ice pack feels good on my sore shoulder. "Why don't you sit with me, and we'll put a movie on?"

He nods, turns on the TV, and passes me the remote. Then he sits next to me with his iPad in his lap.

He often works as I watch television. I won't admit it out loud, but I enjoy just being with him.

And that's stupid. But it is what it is.

"How about *Thor*?" I ask. "The third one. It's the funniest."

"I'm game."

I turn it on and then lean my head on Carmine's strong shoulder. Thor and Hulk are in an arena, about to battle it out as my eyes slip closed, and I fall asleep.

"WAKE UP, PRETTY GIRL."

I take a deep breath and crack open one eye. It's still dark outside. "Jesus, what time is it?"

"Five," he says. He's already fully dressed in a dark suit, no tie. "I told the pilot we'd be in our seats no later than six-thirty."

"Here's your hat. What's your hurry?" I bury my face in my pillow.

"We'll lose three hours to the time change, and I want to see Mick and Billy this afternoon."

Just the mention of the Sergi family makes me groan.

It's been five days since we took our walk, and I almost fell. My shoulder seems to have recovered, and Carmine called Billy Sergi, the second in command there, last night.

They granted him access to the city.

Of course, Carmine didn't say anything about having *me* with him.

I drag my ass out of bed and stumble into the bathroom. After I've done my business and am in the steamy shower, Carmine magically appears with a cup of coffee.

"You're a god," I say as I take the mug and sip the hot brew. "Thanks."

"You're welcome. Be ready in twenty."

He marches out again, but not before his eyes wander over my naked body.

Carmine hasn't made any moves on me in the

weeks we were at the penthouse. He's kept things completely platonic.

And I know that it was *my* insistence that ensured we didn't have sex.

Sex muddies the waters. Clouds judgment.

And sex with Carmine is so fucking good, I would be a quivering pile of sexual need twenty-four-seven if we started something physical.

But damn, I miss the sex. And judging by the look in Carmine's eyes when he walked away, he does, too.

I let the hot water and caffeine wake me up, and thirty minutes later—much to his annoyance—I'm ready to go.

"It's a good thing I packed last night," I say. "Or I would have been late."

His brow lifts, and I can't help but laugh.

I'm back in business-mode, dressed in black slacks, a white silk shirt, and a red scarf. Tall, black Louboutin heels complete the outfit, and when I stand next to Carmine, I'm only a few inches shorter than he is.

"Those shoes do things to me," he mutters.

"I know." I tuck my makeup bag under my arm and follow him into the elevator. When we reach the garage, the driver meets us and tucks our bags into the trunk.

Because it's so early, traffic to the airfield isn't crazy. We don't go to SeaTac. Instead, we're driven to Boeing Field, where many private planes come and go.

The driver parks near the Martinelli jet, and before

long, we're tucked safely inside, coffee at our elbows, and a flight attendant at our beck and call.

I don't like the way she ogles Carmine.

Not that he's *mine.* He's not. But I still don't like it.

"Have you fucked her?" I ask quietly.

He frowns down at me. "Who?"

"Her." I don't look up at the flight attendant.

"Look at me."

I don't do as he asks. I won't look at him and show him the vulnerability in my eyes. It pisses me off that it's there in the first place.

"Nadia."

"Forget I asked. Let's talk about how high-maintenance you are, Carmine. Why can't we just take a commercial flight to New York? First class is pretty swanky these days."

"Your father has a jet."

"Yeah, for *him* to use. The only time I'm on it is if I'm traveling with him. I'm okay with a normal flight."

"Must I remind you that you're carrying a ten-thousand-dollar handbag?"

I glance down at my Birkin and smile. "I never forget about my bag. But it was a gift. And a one-time purchase. It doesn't cost me anything to maintain it."

"You're decked out in luxury brands from head to toe, Nadia. You live well. I won't apologize for doing the same. We all have things we're willing to splurge on. This is one of mine. I fund every flight I take on this jet. Not the family. And because I've been savvy with my money, I can afford the luxury."

"Hey, I'm not irresponsible with my money." I poke him in the side. "I just don't have a fancy portfolio."

"I'm going to help you with that."

"Why would you do that?"

"Because it's important to have investments. It only adds to your independence. And after what you told me about your lack of trust with your family, I think it's imperative that you're dependent on them as little as possible."

I stare at him, my mouth agape. "You're *worried* about me."

He rolls his eyes. "Don't be silly."

"You *like* me," I continue, teasing him. "I think you *like me,* like me, Carmine Martinelli. What will people say?"

"Stop talking."

"The next thing you know, you'll be pledging your undying love and proposing. I don't want to have babies, Carmine. I'm telling you that now—"

The next thing I know, I'm trapped against the back of the seat, and he's kissing the hell out of me. This isn't a playful peck to get me to stop talking. It's passionate, full of frustration and lust, and I hear the moan coming out of my throat as I sink my fingers into his dark hair and hang on tight as he takes me on an erotic ride.

"That'll teach you to shut up when I tell you to," he mutters against my lips as the plane taxis down the runway. "And the answer to your question is, no. I've never fucked her."

I clear my throat as he backs away and returns to his seat, settles in.

"It's none of my business."

"Keep telling yourself that, sweetheart."

"Maybe I should stay here."

We've been in the suite at the Four Seasons for an hour. The space is decorated in black and white, all modern and clean and completely sterile.

It's beautiful, most likely costs a small fortune, and is not my style *at all.*

But I'd rather stay here than head into the lion's den.

"You're not staying here, Nadia."

"I told you before…the Sergi family doesn't like me, Carmine."

That's putting it mildly.

"What did you do, kill one of them?"

"No. I was supposed to marry Billy but I threw a fit, and my father told them never mind. It pissed them off. You know how it is when a family is supposed to marry into another."

"Elena was supposed to marry Alex," he says dryly. "She dodged that bullet."

"Exactly. I dodged the same one. And they're just not happy about it. They don't trust us now."

"When did this happen?"

"Six years ago."

He whistles between his teeth. "That's a long time, Nadia. If all's been quiet since then, I'd think they've moved on and have other things to be mad about."

"Yeah, well, you'd think." I bite my lip. "Still, I'll just hang out here and wait for you."

"No, you'll come with me. But I suggest you change out of those heels."

I shake my head, resigned to my fate. "They're a weapon if I need them. And I can run in them as easily as I can in my sneakers. I also have a concealed sidearm on me."

"Where?"

I smirk. "I'm not telling you that."

He saunters over to me. "Maybe I'll find it for myself later."

"You can try."

His jaw tightens as he looks me over with hungry eyes, but he only swallows and turns away.

"Let's go. The sooner we do this, the quicker we can start asking questions in other areas of the city. This is a courtesy call to say hello and let them know what we're up to."

"Great."

The Sergi's headquarters is located in downtown

Manhattan, right in the middle of all the action. The building looks innocent enough.

But I would bet every cent I have in the bank—which is more than Carmine expects, and that I invested just fine, thank you very much—that the things that happen in this building would turn Carmine's hair white.

I take a deep breath as he holds the door for me. We're shown into an office where Billy and his father Mick sit.

Mick's the boss.

Billy does his bidding.

It's all very customary as far as mafia families go.

"It's good to see you, Mick," Carmine says. But, suddenly, Mick flies to his feet, and guns are drawn, all pointed our way.

"What the fuck is she doing here?"

CHAPTER 6

"Whoa, whoa, whoa." I hold up my hands and slide to my left, closer to Nadia. Jesus, she wasn't kidding.

They really don't like her.

"You didn't say anything about that bitch being here," Mick sneers.

"She's with me," I say quickly. "Our families are working together because we've recently come under attack. I'm here because we need your help."

Mick's eyes narrow, but he signals for his goons to put away their weapons.

"What's going on?" Mick asks.

Billy hasn't said a word. He only glares at Nadia as we step forward into the luxurious office and sit across from Mick.

I briefly fill the boss in on the attempt on my father's life at the wedding in Denver, the subsequent attack on Nadia, and then remind him of my aunt's and uncle's murders long ago.

"Do you honestly think Vinnie's murder is tied to this now?" Mick asks, doubt hanging heavily in his voice.

"I don't know, but I'm going to find out," I reply. "I need to ask around the city, find out what your men know about the attempt on my father's life—and Nadia's for that matter."

"The Martinellis and the Tarenkovs are working together," Mick mutters and shakes his head. "Fascinating. Well, you can ask around, but no one will tell you anything. Even if they do know what's going on. This isn't your territory."

"Then what do you suggest?"

"Go home," he says bluntly.

"Not without answers."

Mick blows out a long breath. "We should have had this conversation over the phone. If you'd given me a heads-up, I could have asked around before you got here."

"There's a lot to be said for looking into a man's eyes when you talk to him." I clear my throat. "Mick, *you* aren't behind this, are you?"

"No." His lips flatten into a hard line. "It's true, there is no love lost between our family and the Tarenkovs, but my beef isn't worth a war. And Carlo and I have always had an agreeable relationship. But, if you'll give me a couple of days, I'll ask around. On the down-low.

I don't think it's wise to bring a lot of attention to this. It might escalate the situation or make those responsible go into hiding. And then you'll never get your answers."

I nod in agreement. He hasn't said anything that I didn't already take into consideration.

"It looks like Nadia and I will spend a few days in your beautiful city. Take in the sights. Maybe see a show."

"Enjoy your vacation," Mick advises. "I'll be in touch when I know something."

"Thank you." We rise and start to leave, but turn back at Mick's voice.

"The next time you request entry into my city, you'd better be fucking honest about who you're bringing with you. I don't like surprises."

"Understood."

"I'VE HEARD great things about this show." Nadia walks out of the walk-in closet off our suite's bedroom and holds the necklace I gave her in Denver out to me. "Will you please fasten this?"

"Of course." I slip the diamonds and platinum around her slim neck and fasten it under her hairline, then kiss the ball of her shoulder. I notice she doesn't have any earrings in. "You're damn beautiful, Nadia."

She grins at me and then does a little spin in her red

dress, showing it off. "Thanks. I'm glad I brought this along, just in case. And you look pretty damn good yourself in that suit."

I adjust the knot of my tie and then hold my hand out for hers. "Shall we?"

"Let me just grab my clutch." She rushes to the bed and slips a tube of lipstick into her bag, then takes my proffered hand. "Let's go watch a Broadway show."

The truth is, Nadia takes my breath away. She handled herself well at Mick's office today, knowing when to stay quiet and let me do the talking. She's intelligent. And she's sexy as fuck.

I shouldn't have kissed her on the plane this morning. I was only trying to shut her up, but all I did was remind myself how good we are together in bed.

How much I want her.

How I never *stopped* wanting her.

And she's made it clear that a physical relationship is out of the question.

I'm a damn fool. I need to keep my hands to myself and keep my focus on the task at hand.

She's a colleague who has become a friend. That's all.

But when we step into the elevator, and she leans her head on my shoulder as we watch the floors tick down, all I want to do is pull her to me and kiss her breathless.

Instead, I turn my lips down and kiss the top of her head.

"Tell me about this show." *Before I take you back upstairs and fuck you into next week.*

"The lead actress is London Watson. She's a *huge* name in theater, and she wrote this show a couple of years ago. Still stars in it. I'm excited to finally see it."

"Sounds great."

We walk through the hotel lobby and see our car is waiting. The ride through Manhattan is slow, as always, but before long, the driver drops us off in front of the theater. I bought us VIP tickets, so we bypass the line and are immediately shown to our seats.

"That's Paul Rudd," Nadia whispers and nods to the man several seats down. "Holy shit, I love *Ant-Man.*"

"Tell him so. We have a few minutes before the show starts."

She bites her lip and then shrugs her shoulder and stands to approach the actor. Paul smiles up at her, then stands to talk to her. I can't hear everything that's said, but there are smiles, a couple of laughs, and then Nadia returns to me.

"Oh my God," she says. "He's so nice."

"He looked like a good guy."

She grins. "This is a fun day. Well, aside from having guns pointed at my face, of course."

"Yeah, that was a little intense."

"But the rest of it has been better than expected."

"I'm glad."

She links her arm through mine and leans on me. Nadia has become more and more physically affectionate over the past few weeks, at least since we started staying at the penthouse again.

I don't mind the affection.

But damn if it doesn't make me want more.

"You really do look nice in this suit," she says casually. "I don't think I've seen it before."

"I'm sure you have."

"No, this one is navy. You usually wear black."

I glance down at her. "You pay attention to the color of my suits?"

"You usually wear black," she says again. "I like this on you."

The lights flicker, signaling the start of the show. Through the entire three hours, Nadia touches me—holds my hand, leans her head on my shoulder, smiles up at me.

She's flirting with me.

Blatantly.

Boldly.

Either she's trying to seduce me, or she's playing a game. And I have no patience for that. She has me tied in knots, my dick semi-hard as we leave the theater.

"London was *amazing*," she gushes as we get into the waiting car. "She's so talented. I absolutely loved it. Man, I'm starving."

She grins over at me.

"Are you hungry?"

"Hmm."

She frowns. "You don't know if you're hungry?"

"I could use something." I turn my head and watch Manhattan pass us by. The traffic is no less frantic at midnight than it was close to four hours ago.

"Let's just order in at the hotel," she suggests. "We can get comfortable and eat all the food. That sounds awesome."

I nod. When the car stops in front of the Four Seasons, a bellman opens our door. I climb out first, then turn to offer Nadia my hand to help her out of the vehicle.

She's in another pair of those mile-high heels she loves. The kind that look damn hot over my shoulders as I fuck her into oblivion.

I remember very well.

"New York just energizes me," she says when we step into the elevator. "Don't you love this city?"

"You're talkative tonight," is my only reply.

"It's New York," she says. "Like I said, it energizes me. I don't come here often enough. For obvious reasons."

She slides her hand into mine, and I glance down at her.

"Why are you flirting with me so hard tonight?"

Her smile doesn't dim, but the light in her blue eyes sparks. "Oh, so you *did* notice?"

"Hard not to." I lead her out of the elevator and down the long hallway to the presidential suite, then unlock the door and walk inside. "You've turned it up."

"Turned what up?"

"The flirting." I turn and look at her as I loosen my tie. She drops her bag onto a table and crosses her arms over her chest. "What's going on?"

"I like flirting with you." She moves to me and brushes my hands out of the way so she can unbutton my shirt. "I like *being* with you."

"You set the rules hard and fast from the beginning of this, Nadia. No sex. I've upheld my end of that bargain."

"I know." There's no flirtation in her voice now as her eyes find mine. "And I also know that it's unfair and just plain ridiculous to muddy the waters. To change the rules."

"But I have a feeling you're going to do just that."

"We're good together," she says at last. "I thought I could turn that piece off. That I could ignore it. But damn it, the truth is, we *are* good together. And we'll be working together for God knows how long."

"Are you saying that you want to reintroduce sex into our dynamic?"

"Well, that just sounds like a business merger." She rises onto her tiptoes and barely skims her lips over mine. "And there's nothing sexy about a business merger. What you and I do to each other is fucking sexy, Carmine."

I sigh, wanting nothing more in this moment than *her.* And in about six seconds, I'm going to have her.

But we need to get something straight first.

"There's no pretense here, Nadia. No act."

"It's just you and me, who we *really* are, enjoying each other, Carmine. I know that."

"Good."

I don't waste any time. I lift her against me and hurry to the bedroom. "If anything hurts—"

"Trust me, this doesn't hurt."

I grin and set her on her feet next to the bed. "Leave the shoes on."

Her eyes are full of pure female satisfaction as she reaches behind her and unzips the dress, letting it pool around her ankles.

"Leave the necklace on, too."

"Any other requests?"

I laugh and urge her back onto the bed. "No. Let me do the rest." I take her right foot in my hand and kiss her ankle bone, right above the shoe. "Do you have any idea what these fucking shoes do to me?"

"Why do you think I wear them?"

She leans back on her hands, watching me as I kiss up her leg, then spread her wide and lick a wet trail from her inner thigh to the pink lips of her glistening pussy.

"You were always good at this."

She sighs and lays back on the mountain of pillows as I take her on the ride of her life—all with my mouth. I lick and suck, then lick some more. I vary the pressure and speed, and when I push two fingers inside of her, she comes apart spectacularly.

"Good girl," I murmur as I kiss up her flat stomach to her breasts. "I love your tits. You know that, right?"

"They never grew in."

"Excuse me?"

She laughs and brushes her hand through my hair. "When I was young, I was desperate for them to grow so boys would notice me. Much to my dismay, they stayed small."

"I see zero things wrong with these." I brush my tongue over a hard peek and then kiss her neck passionately.

I fumble in the bedside drawer, find a little packet, and make quick work of protecting us. But before I can slide home, she pushes me onto my back and straddles my hips.

She always loved this position the best, and she'll get no complaints from me.

She rides me hard and fast and reaches back to cup my already-tight balls.

"Fuck, Nadia."

"Yes, fuck Nadia," she agrees and clenches her core around me.

I don't want to come yet, so I grip her hips in my hands, lift her, then shift our position so I'm behind her. Then, I push back inside. Her round ass is in the air, and I give it a loud smack as I fuck her from behind.

"God, Carmine." She clenches the bedsheets in her fists and pushes back against me. "Yes."

Three more hard thrusts are all it takes to have us both coming apart at the seams, crying out in ecstasy.

"OH, GOD, I LOVE THIS."

She's wearing a white hotel robe and nothing else, and we're sitting on the terrace, a large tray of food on the table between us as she eats her weight in shrimp cocktail.

"I mean, just look at the lights."

The New York lights are stunning. We're not far from the World Trade Center memorial and can even see the lights of it from here.

"It's a beautiful place," I agree and reach for a taco. Tacos aren't on the menu, but they made them for me tonight. "If you love it here so much, why don't you live here?"

"Because I'm a Tarenkov," she reminds me. "There's no way the Sergis would allow that. Especially Billy. That little worm."

She sips her chocolate shake and scowls.

"He did seem a bit angry with you today."

She laughs at that and then switches from her shrimp to the dessert she ordered: crème brûlée.

"He's a baby. Worse than Alex," she says as an afterthought. "I would keep an apartment here in a heartbeat, but it's not possible because of the family drama. The Sergis don't trust us, and we don't trust them either, truth be told. But once a year, I do come shopping. I send Mick an email, and he always replies cordially, giving me a four-day pass to spend some time here. It's the best four days of my year."

"This is still a free country, Nadia."

She turns sad, blue eyes up at me. "Come on, Carmine. You know that isn't true for people like us. Never has been. Men who claim to love us dictate our lives, but they wouldn't hesitate to use us for personal gain if they saw the need arise. It's a game we play every damn day of our lives."

She eats more of her dessert.

"But you know what? I don't want to talk about that."

"What do you want to talk about?"

"I don't want to chat at all. I want to lick what's left of this crème brûlée off your penis."

My eyebrows climb at the suggestion. "I'm not saying no."

"I didn't think you would."

CHAPTER 7

~NADIA~

I wake up in the center of maybe the biggest bed on Earth, all of the blankets rumpled and in a pile in the middle, with me draped around them like the big spoon.

Carmine, however, is nowhere to be found.

I sit up and rub the sleep from my eyes. I'm sure I have mascara shadows under my lashes because I didn't bother washing my face before Carmine carried me in here and had his way with me.

I grin and stand, feeling the pull of tender muscles. The soreness feels good, though, not at all like it did as I recovered from the attack. I feel good and sexed.

I pad naked into the living space to see if Carmine is reading the news on his iPad, but he's not out here, either. So, I walk into the half-bath in the hall, use the restroom, and then find the white robe on the floor where Carmine let it fall, wrapping it around myself.

I journey back through the bedroom to the master bath and lean on the doorjamb with a grin.

Lounging in the white porcelain soaking tub is Carmine, up to his neck in sudsy water. He's laid his head back, and his eyes are closed.

I cross to him and let my robe fall to the floor.

"Don't you smell nice?" I murmur. He opens his eyes. They immediately warm, then travel the length of me. "Looks like there's room for two."

"Why don't we find out?"

I grin and climb into the hot water, straddling his hips and rubbing myself against him playfully. "I didn't peg you as a bath guy."

"It feels good to soak now and then."

I sniff the air. "Is that rose oil, I smell?"

"What's wrong with a little rose oil?"

I lean over to bite his neck. "Like I said yesterday, you're just a little high-maintenance."

"I like luxurious things," he says, but his voice doesn't sound defensive. He's simply stating a fact. "Whether that's a private jet or a soak in a tub the size of Manhattan, it doesn't matter."

I push my wet hand through his hair. "I just like to give you shit."

"If you keep rubbing yourself on me like that, I'll give you something, too."

"Oh?" I cock an eyebrow and grind on him. "Like this?"

"You're a vixen," he mutters. "And it would take a saint to resist you."

"I have it on good authority that you're no saint."

He laughs and glides his hands up my thighs to my waist and then around to my ass, cupping the globes and lifting me gently so he can urge his cock inside of me.

"No condom," he growls.

"Still on the pill." My voice is raspy. The water sloshes around us as I start to move. God, I love this position. The head of his dick glides perfectly over my most sensitive places, sending thrilling shockwaves through me.

I never last long when I ride him, and with the water caressing my ass, my sides, and my lower back, I come faster than ever, crying out with each wave that hits me.

"Again," he orders. "Look at me."

His brown eyes are hot as he works me harder and faster. He's sitting up now, guiding me, pushing me until we both succumb to a climax that has us shivering and panting.

"Well, okay then." I swallow hard. "Good morning."

"Yes, it is." He nuzzles my breasts, then leans back against the tub once more. "What shall we do today?"

"Are you kidding me? I'm in New York. I want to go shopping."

His grin is wide and full of humor.

"I was hoping you'd say that."

I stand and carefully step out of the tub. I don't want to fall on my ass, and we spilled a lot of water during our fun time.

"I need a shower, but I'll be ready in an hour."

"I'll order up breakfast," he says as he climbs out of the tub.

"It's handy having you around, Carmine."

He grins, winks at me, and then leaves the bathroom.

Jesus, Mary, and Joseph, that man is sexy. I start the shower, and when the water is the right temperature, I step in and get busy washing my face.

I'm in a damn good mood. Maybe the best I've been in for months. Maybe ever. I'm in my favorite city, with someone I enjoy, and I'm going to spend an obscene amount of money.

"Breakfast will be here in twenty," Carmine calls out.

"Sounds good," I yell back.

Yeah, it's damn convenient having that man around.

"The bag you just bought looks like the one you already have."

We're eating pizza and sitting by a fountain. The boutiques will deliver our new things to the Four Seasons for us so we don't have to walk around Manhattan loaded down with bags.

"Uh, excuse me Mr. I-just-bought-a-ten-thousand-dollar-watch-that-looks-just-like-the-one-I'm-currently-wearing."

He stops mid-chew and narrows his eyes at me. "It looks nothing like this watch."

"And my new bag looks nothing like the others I have." I shrug a shoulder. "Besides, it's a new style this season. And it's going to look *so* cute with jeans and a sweater."

"I want to look at shoes at Bergdorf."

I grin at him. "I can live with that."

We finish our pizza and walk down the street to the old store, wandering through. Browsing. When we find the men's shoes, Carmine studies some Louboutins that have me salivating.

He's not the only one who appreciates luxury.

"You could wear those with any and all of your suits."

He nods and wanders down the table, picking up a pair of sneakers. Carmine flags down a salesperson and asks to try them on in his size.

"Sneakers?"

"I do wear casual clothes."

I take in his khaki slacks and light blue button-down. "When?"

"I brought out a couple of sizes because you just never know how Louboutins will fit," the salesman says as he returns and sets the boxes at Carmine's feet.

After twenty minutes—and six pairs—Carmine

chooses two, and then we're off to find the women's shoe section, just one floor up.

"I need more heels like I need a hole in the head," I mutter as I brush my index finger over a pair of glossy patent leather Chanel heels. "But damn if they're not beautiful."

I try on Dior, Choo, and Hermes, and settle on a pair of Dior slingbacks, Hermes sneakers, and the *cutest* Valentino flip-flops.

Again, they'll deliver everything to our room, so we leave the store and start walking down Fifth, hand in hand, enjoying the afternoon sun.

"I did a lot of damage today," I say with a happy sigh. "But it's so fun. Nothing compares to shopping in New York. Well, aside from Paris. Paris is the mecca, of course. But New York ranks up there. I could have spent all day in the Hermes boutique and bought scarves and all kinds of fun little things. But I won't wear them often, so I need to be strong and cut myself off."

"I enjoy watching you shop. You touch everything."

"I'm a texture girl. I like to feel the leathers, the silks, and cashmeres. It *feels* pretty, you know?"

"Just one of the reasons I enjoy touching you."

I laugh, but when I look up at him, he's staring down at me, and he is *not* laughing. "You're charming, you know that?"

"I'm just telling the truth. I hope you like tea."

"Tea?"

He nods and leads me to the doorway of the Tiffany & Co. We get in the elevator and ride it to the fourth floor, and then he leads me to the Blue Box Café.

"Oh, I've never eaten there."

"We're having afternoon tea," he informs me with a smile.

"Fancy."

A regal woman with perfectly coifed, sable hair greets us. She takes Carmine's name and checks her reservation list, then leads us to our table and sets Tiffany-blue menus in front of us.

"We're having the afternoon tea," Carmine informs her.

"Of course." She nods and backs away. What seems like only moments later, a waiter wheels a cart to our table, piled high with finger foods and hot, steeping tea.

The waiter explains everything on the tray, pours us each a cup, and then leaves us to our own devices.

"I'm sort of shocked," I admit as I reach for a scone, break it in half, and spread real, whipped butter on it.

"At what?"

"This is the last thing I would have expected from you."

"We've had plenty of meals together."

"I meant the *tea*." I chuckle and take a bite of my scone, then close my eyes in happiness. "This is delicious."

"We'd already had lunch, but I wanted to do something different for you."

"This is different. And fun. And fancy."

I watch as his brows knit together.

"It's okay, Carmine. I like the fancy side of you."

We try the finger sandwiches, some fruit, and spend an hour simply enjoying each other's company.

"This place is just so beautiful." I look over at the wall with an enormous clock on it. The wall itself looks as if it's made of gray and Tiffany-blue granite. "And the food was great."

I yawn and cover my mouth with my napkin.

"Am I boring you?" he asks.

"No. Definitely, not." I laugh and run my fingers through my hair. "I think all the walking and shopping is finally catching up with me. Maybe it's time to head back and catch a nap."

"We have one more stop to make first."

I tilt my head. "Where?"

"It isn't far."

He pays the check and then pulls me through the restaurant and back into the elevator, but rather than leave the store, he leads me to a waiting salesperson.

"Hello, sir," the man says with a slight bow. "I'm Dennis. I'll be happy to work with you today."

I frown at Carmine. "Looking for another watch?"

"Earrings," he says as Dennis starts to pull velvet boxes out of the glass cases and sets them on the counter. "You weren't wearing any earrings when we went to the theater last night."

I stare up at him. "Seriously?"

He quirks a brow. "I'm quite sure Dennis would be rather upset if I were kidding." He turns to the other man. "Did you see the necklace?"

"My necklace?"

Dennis nods. "I received your text with the photo. It's a stunning piece, and I'm sure we have earrings here that will match it nicely."

"You want me to pick out earrings to match my necklace?"

I stare at him, blinking slowly, dumbfounded.

"That's why we're here," he says.

"You don't have to do that."

"Give us a moment," he says, and Dennis discretely walks away so we can talk in private.

"Carmine, you don't have to buy me gifts."

"I don't have to do much of anything," he says. "I *want* to do this for you. They'll look beautiful."

"You gave me a lot of gifts when we were fake-dating." I chew my lower lip.

"We're not fake anything now," he says smoothly and reaches out to brush his thumb across the apple of my cheek. "I enjoy you, Nadia. More than I anticipated. And I'd like to buy you something beautiful to remember our time in New York. No strings attached."

What if I'm starting to wish for strings?

My heart flutters. What the fuck is wrong with me?

Carmine signals for Dennis to rejoin us, and I turn to the several velvet trays with a sigh.

I know as soon as my eyes land on them.

They're understated, which works well because the necklace is anything but. These earrings won't overshadow the diamonds around my neck but will add just a bit of sparkle to my ears.

"These."

Dennis offers them to me, along with a mirror, and I fasten them onto my lobes, then tilt my head side to side, admiring them.

"Would you like to look at the chandeliers?" Dennis asks, pointing to a gorgeous pair of diamond earrings that probably cost about the same as a small suburban home.

"No, thanks." I turn to Carmine. His lips are tipped up in a small smile. "These will go perfectly."

"I think you're right."

He reaches out and touches my ear with his finger. "Discreet, but beautiful."

"And the necklace is still the centerpiece."

"No." He steps into me and lowers his lips to my ear. "*You're* the centerpiece, sweetheart. The jewelry is just frosting."

He turns back to Dennis.

"We'll take them."

"Excellent, sir."

Dennis is all smiles as he sees to the bill, and I can't stop hearing the last words from Carmine in my head.

The rest is just frosting.

Has anyone taken the time to see me for *me*? To see past the designer clothes and accessories to the woman beneath? I feel like I've been constantly trying to prove to my father, my brother, and everyone in our family that I'm smart enough and damn savvy enough to take over the organization one day.

But they always dismiss me.

Not Carmine. He respects my opinions and listens to me when I talk. He acknowledges that I enjoy pretty things but also knows that it's just the surface.

That what's beneath is so much more.

"Ready?" he asks with a smile.

"Yes." I look in the mirror once more, happy to wear the earrings out of the store. "You know, I hope you realize that when I give you shit for being a diva, I don't really mean it."

He glances at me as we walk through the store. "You've never called me a *diva*."

"Not in those words, exactly."

"Does it truly bother you that I like the finer things? Does it emasculate me in your eyes?"

"No." Visions of Carmine and I in bed swim in my head. Of him working out. Of all the ways that he shows, every day, that he's a *man*. One I'm incredibly attracted to. "Not at all."

"Good, because I plan to take you back to the hotel and fuck you blind."

My mouth opens and closes. I'm not sure what in the hell to say to that.

But when we step outside, four men suddenly surround us, all with weapons drawn.

"The boss wants to see you. Get in the car."

I sigh and frown at all four of them. "What in the hell is it with the Sergi organization and guns? Can't you just ask a girl nicely?"

"Let's go," the goon says, ignoring my statement altogether. "You can complain about how we do things to the boss."

CHAPTER 8

~CARMINE~

"You do realize that it's not necessary to hold us at gunpoint to get us into your office." My voice is dry as I sit across from Mick and narrow my eyes at him. "We're happy to come in willingly."

Mick smiles, but his eyes aren't full of humor.

"I have no idea what you're talking about."

I just stare back at him until he looks down at the papers on his desk. "I've done some asking around, some talking, and I'm afraid I don't know much more than you do."

"But you know something."

Mick leans back in his chair and folds his beefy hands over his impressive stomach. When you think of the stereotypical mob boss, Mick is the image that comes to most minds. He's a big man—in both stature and weight. He's imposing.

"Turns out, someone approached one of my men about selling something new here in the city."

I sit forward. "A new drug?"

"Yeah, but I don't know who did the approaching. Or what kind of drug."

I scowl. "Come on, Mick, you know everything that goes on in New York."

The other man's eyes flash with anger. "I thought I did. And trust me when I say that I'd be happy to drag my man in here to interrogate him myself."

"Then do it."

"He's fucking dead."

"Goddamn it." I rub my hand over my mouth. "How did he die?"

"I was at that wedding," Mick reminds me. "My man has been dead for a few days, but it looks like he met the same fate your father's man did."

"Poison," Nadia murmurs beside me. "Are they trying to sell poison? Why would anyone take it if the result is death?"

"I don't think it's the poison they want to sell," Mick says. "There've been rumblings of something new on the streets. Something damn powerful, addictive, and cheap to make."

"Hell, you just described meth," Carmine says.

"I'm not a fan of drugs," Mick replies. "I know some of my guys sell a little here and there, but that's not my game. And they know it. My hunch is that my guy told the stranger no, and that answer wasn't the right one. I have no way of knowing who it was that approached him."

"His cell?" I ask, already knowing the answer.

"Gone." Mick hisses out a breath. "Listen, this doesn't sit well with me, either. Someone came, unannounced, into my city and killed my man. I'm damn pissed."

"I know the feeling." I stare at Mick. "What now?"

"I'll keep asking," Mick says. "You keep me posted, as well. Someone's going to pay for this."

"On that, we can agree. I'll keep you informed when and if we find anything. I appreciate you working with us on this, rather than against us."

"It seems someone has decided to wage war with several organizations," Mick says thoughtfully. "They're either very brave or out of their fucking minds."

"Maybe both," Nadia adds, and Mick's eyes slide over to her for the first time.

"We'll stay in touch," Mick says again, dismissing us.

"Thanks for your time." We stand, and before I can walk away, Mick says my name.

"Carmine. Watch your back. This has *conspiracy* written all over it."

"Same to you."

"I GUESS THIS WAS A WASTED TRIP," Nadia says as she flops onto the sofa in our suite.

"Not at all."

I sit next to her and lift her feet into my lap. "We had a good few days here. And although it's not the information we were hoping for, we at least know it's not Mick."

"He could be lying."

I stare at her pink-tipped toes as I push my thumb into the arch of her foot. "I don't think so. He's pissed."

"What now?"

I've been running that question through my mind since we left Mick's office. "I think we need to go back to the city where this all started."

"Denver."

I nod and reach out to brush her hair behind her ear just as my phone rings.

"Hi, Shane."

"Hey, what did you find out from Mick?"

I relay the information and hear my brother curse on the other end of the line. "Yeah, that was my thought, exactly."

"This is a game for someone," Shane says. "They're fucking playing with us. But why? What's the end game?"

"That's the million-dollar question," I reply. "Nadia and I are headed to Denver first thing in the morning. I think we need to do some digging there."

"Denver is supposed to be neutral ground for all of the families," Shane reminds me.

"Yeah, well, that went in the toilet when someone tried to kill Pop."

"I'll meet you there," Shane says. "See you at the office."

"See you."

I hang up and turn to Nadia, who's watching me closely.

"Shane's going to meet us in Denver. He's been at his place in the mountains for the past couple of weeks, doing some digging of his own."

"Why does he have a place in Colorado?"

I tilt my head to the side. "Why shouldn't he?"

"Denver is neutral ground. We all have offices there, but no one lives there."

"Your cousin and her husband do," I remind her. "Just because your father isn't based there full time doesn't mean he doesn't have connections to the city. Besides, Shane doesn't live *in* Denver. He lives in a small mountain town called Victor, several hours outside the city."

"Shane's been there this whole time?"

I narrow my eyes at her. "He's a grown man and can live anywhere he likes, Nadia. Shane likes solitude. The mountains suit him. And he's within driving distance to several airports and can get in and out easily."

"Hmm," is all she says as the doorbell rings. "Oh, I bet that's our stuff."

She hurries to the door, and sure enough, it's the bellman with all of our purchases on a cart. He unloads them onto the dining table big enough to seat eight, then leaves. Nadia is all smiles as she starts digging into bags and boxes wrapped with ribbon.

"I'm *so* glad I got these shoes," she says as she slips out of her sneakers and tries on her new Dior heels."

"What's your problem with my brothers?" I ask while she's in a good mood and on a new shoe high.

"I don't know them well," she replies. "Oh, I forgot about this jacket. I know it's summer, but it'll be perfect for fall."

"But you don't like Shane having property in Colorado."

She shrugs a shoulder as she checks out her new purchase in a full-length mirror. "It's just all suspect. Shane has a place near Denver. This mess started in Denver."

"Your cousin lives in Colorado," I remind her once more. "All of the families have offices there. Just because Shane spends more time there than most doesn't make him the cause of all of this."

"I know." She sighs and turns back to me. "And I also know that you care about him, and you'd defend him to the ground."

"Every fucking day," I agree, frustration a bubble in my throat. "If we're all going to be judged by our taste in real estate, Annika and her husband could be the cause of all this, too. The first attack happened at their wedding, after all."

"Oh, come on." She turns to me as she lets the jacket fall off her arms and catches it with her fingers. "Rich is an ear, nose, and throat doctor. He's no mobster. And he certainly isn't a drug dealer."

"Annika?"

Her eyes flash in temper and annoyance.

Good, we're on equal footing.

"Annika has worked her ass off to stay out of the family business. She wants no part of it. None of it. She's a damn good doctor. Hell, *I'm* more likely to be the one behind this than she is."

I cock a brow.

"No. It's not me."

"Well, it's not me, either. At least, we've established that. Let's get to Denver in the morning. We can plan what happens next then."

She blows out a breath and reaches for her Chanel shopping bag. "Okay. In the meantime, I'm going to play with my new goodies."

"Play away, sweetheart."

"Rocco." I smile at my brother as Nadia and I walk into our Denver offices. "I wasn't expecting to see you here."

"Shane called me last night. I want in on the fun." He nods at Nadia. "Hi."

"Hello. *Rafe*."

My brother rolls his eyes. I don't know why he doesn't care for his given name, but he's always insisted that people call him Rocco, ever since he was a kid.

Of course, Mom refuses to call him anything but Rafe. She named him after one of her favorite characters in a romance novel.

Maybe *that's* why he doesn't like it.

"I have something," Shane says as he hurries through the door. "And let me just say, it wasn't easy to get."

"What is it?" I ask as he sits at the desk and opens his laptop, then starts tapping the keys.

"The waiter from the wedding." Shane's brow furrows as he searches the screen. "No one knew who he was. I asked the catering company. They had no record of him. I had to bust into the security camera logs at the resort. And let me just tell you, their security is buttoned down *tight*. Took me several days to crack the code.

"But once I did, I was able to find some footage of our man. Here." He points to the screen. "See him? He's floating through the crowd a bit."

"It's grainy and in black and white," I say, squinting to see better.

"Yeah, their security is the bomb, but the video quality sucks. I cleaned it up a bit."

He points to the bigger monitor on the desk, and Rocco, Nadia, and I shift our attention there.

"Carmine and Nadia sneak off," Shane says with a cheeky smile. "You look a little intense there, brother."

I was. I wanted to fuck Nadia like I'd never wanted anything else in my whole damn life. And if memory serves, it was some pretty damn good sex.

Nadia glances up at me with a smirk.

"Okay. Here." Shane points to the screen. "See, he's setting the glass for Pop on the table."

"And looking around while he does it," Nadia adds. "That's definitely shady."

"None of us noticed," Rocco says. "We were all too busy partying."

"Our guards were down because it was supposed to be neutral territory," I say, thinking it over. "Not just in Denver, but at the wedding. We all had our guards down."

"Before Pop can take a sip, Armando takes the glass by accident. He's laughing with someone and just picks it up and drinks."

I watch as Armando does just that. Pop looks over and scowls for a second, then shrugs and laughs, signaling for a waiter to order a fresh drink.

"I'm going to speed this up a bit because it takes a couple of minutes for the poison to kick in." Shane hits a button, and the video runs faster. Then he slows it down, and Armando's face changes. He reaches for his throat, his eyes bulge, and the next thing we see, he's flailing about and ends up in the middle of the dance floor, seizing.

"That's enough," I say, but Shane shakes his head.

"Watch here." He points again. "There's our man. He takes a picture of the scene and then slips back into the crowd. And he doesn't come back. He ducks out."

"You said you found out who he is?" I ask, seeing red.

"Sean Brown," Shane says. "At least, that's the name he's gone by for a while. I found him doing a search for his image. He's also gone by Clark Brown and Rudy Brown."

"Why all the names?" Nadia wants to know.

"He's been in and out of jail," Shane says. "I assume he changes his name so he can get jobs. Have a clean record."

"He's anything but clean. Fuck, he's a contract killer."

"Looks like it," Shane agrees. "I have an address."

"What are we doing sitting here, then?" Rocco pulls his nine-millimeter out of his shoulder holster and checks the magazine. I do the same, and I notice Nadia pulling her small piece from her Hermes bag, checking it, as well.

I laugh.

"What?" she says.

"You carry a concealed in an eleven-thousand-dollar handbag?"

She grins. "Doesn't everyone?"

"WE DON'T KILL HIM." My voice is firm with the order. "We question him."

"Maybe break his arm," Rocco says with a shrug as we climb the steps to the upstairs apartment. Sean—or whatever his name is—lives on the second floor of a rundown building in a shitty part of town.

I raise my fist to knock on the door, but it's ajar.

"Not a good sign," Shane murmurs as he pulls his weapon. We all follow suit, and I nudge the door open with my toe. We soundlessly hurry inside.

But we don't have to go far.

"Fucking hell," I mutter and stare up at the man who used to be Sean as he swings from a noose tied to a beam in the ceiling.

"Shit." Nadia circles around him. "He's been up there a while."

His face is purple, eyes bulged, and the rope cut the hell out of his neck. The smell of decay is overwhelming.

"There's a note," Rocco says and begins to read aloud.

I can't live with what I did. I've done some fucked-up things but killing ain't one of them.

"That's it," Rocco says.

"Well, damn." I rub my hand over my face and listen as Shane murmurs into his phone. He's calling in a cleanup crew.

The cops won't find Sean.

He won't be found at all.

And we're at another dead end, literally. Back to square one. Which royally pisses me off.

"Look for a phone," I say, already headed back to the one and only bedroom in the flop. His phone is on a charger by the bed, so I pocket it. Shane can dig into it when we get back to the office.

I rummage through drawers but don't find anything else when Nadia pokes her head in.

"You'll want to see this."

I follow her to the bathroom and snarl. "Jesus fucking Christ, this is disgusting."

"Yeah, our boy didn't know what a toilet brush is. But that's not what I wanted to show you." She opens the medicine cabinet. "Look at these."

Bags and bags of little blue pills.

"I'll give you two guesses what these are," she says.

"Given that none of us are pharmacists, it could be anything. Maybe Sean had an Aleve habit."

Nadia rolls her eyes. "Right. It's an anti-inflammatory. That's why he had like five thousand of them in this cabinet."

"We'll take them," Shane says. "Crew's on the way. Let's bail."

We take the bags of pills with us, and I skirt by the body still hanging in the living room.

"He looks like a baby."

"Twenty-two," Shane confirms. "Still wet behind the ears."

"Seasoned enough to kill," I remind him. "I'd hardly call him innocent."

CHAPTER 9

~NADIA~

I'm fucking tired.

It's late. Carmine and I left New York before the sun came up this morning, and we've been working hard all day.

Carmine's still at the office with his brothers, but I bailed. I need to sleep. I have to get my mind off drugs and death for a few hours.

I need a break.

I fill the tub in the master bathroom of the beautiful Airbnb Carmine rented and add some bath salts to the water. Before I can strip down and sink in, my phone rings.

Why would Alex be calling me this late?

It's midnight in Atlanta.

"Is Papa okay?" I ask in way of greeting.

"As far as I know," he says. "Can't a guy just call his sister to check in?"

"Not usually. No." I lean my butt on the counter and stare at the water in the tub, wondering what he wants. "What's up?"

"I'm wondering how you're doing. Found anything yet?"

"Not really. We're back in Denver."

"Yes, I heard."

My eyes narrow. "How?"

"We have eyes everywhere, Nadia. You know that. You're still with Carmine."

"Yes."

"Are you still fucking him?"

I don't even know this man anymore. When we were kids, we were close. I adored him. But the older he got, the colder he became.

"You realize you basically just called me a whore?"

"Answer the question, Nadia."

"No, Alexander. I won't. Because I'm a grown woman, on a job given to me by the boss, who doesn't happen to be *you*."

"You're such a bitch. Just tell me what's going on there. Keep me in the damn loop. I can't help if I don't know what's happening."

"I don't want or need any help from you," I counter. "I never have before, and I definitely don't need you now. Just keep your nose and your fingers out of this."

"Nadia—"

I hang up before he can say more.

The water has grown cold, so I drain it and think

about starting over. But I'm too tired, and I've lost interest.

Instead, I start the shower and get in, quickly washing the day away, and then step into leggings and a sweatshirt.

I stop by the kitchen and pour a glass of Cabernet, then scoop up my laptop and walk into the living room.

The sofa faces a wall of windows. It's dark now, but during the day, you can see the mountains to the west.

Carmine has a thing for beautiful views.

I've just opened the laptop and started going through some unanswered emails when Carmine walks through the front door, also looking tired.

But my eyes zero in on the box in his right hand.

"Is that what I think it is?"

He sets the container on the kitchen island, tosses his keys next to it, and glances at me. "I thought you'd enjoy some donuts for breakfast."

"I'd enjoy some donuts *now*."

I laugh and launch off the sofa with renewed energy at the promise of sugar but stop short when I get a good look at Carmine.

"What's wrong?"

He shakes his head and walks to the fridge, pulls out a bottle of beer I didn't know we had, and takes a long pull from the bottle.

"Did something else happen?"

"No." He swallows another sip and then sits on one

of the stools. "It really shouldn't be this hard. I feel like I'm on another wild goose chase, just missing the mark by an inch. It's damn frustrating."

"I know. But we'll figure it out. People are loyal, but I've also found that they like to run their mouths. Someone will fuck up and say something they shouldn't, and we'll find them."

"It's odd for a family to target another and not be bold about it. To stand up and say, '*Yeah, motherfucker, I did this. And I'll do it again.*'"

"The mafia has arrogance down to a science," I agree with a laugh.

"Well, they're not copping to anything now."

I open the box and immediately salivate at the sight of a maple bar. I grab for it like a kid starved to within an inch of her life.

"These are my favorite donuts in the city." I wander over and sit on the couch, chewing happily. "Oh, by the way, we're having dinner at Annika and Rich's place tomorrow."

"We are?" he asks.

"Yep. She called earlier. Your brothers are also invited."

He nods and then wanders to me, leaning in to take a bite of my donut.

"Hey, get your own."

"No." He takes my hand, pulls me to my feet, and leads me to the bedroom. "Now, I want to taste you. You're much more delicious than any donut."

"Lead the way."

ANNIKA AND RICH'S home in the Cherry Creek neighborhood of Denver is beautiful. It's an upscale area that professional sports players, celebrities, and the wealthy in general call home.

And I can see why. In addition to a nice golf course with a country club, there is excellent shopping, restaurants, and bars. If I lived in Denver, this is where I'd buy a house.

"Hi, you guys," Annika says with a wide smile as she opens the front door and gestures for us to come inside. "I'm so excited to see you all."

"You're gorgeous," I say as I lean in to kiss my cousin's cheek. But when I pull back, I can see the tension around her gorgeous blue eyes. I narrow mine, but she shakes her head quickly, sending me a silent message that now isn't the time for that conversation.

She greets Carmine and Shane, and when she reaches Rafe, she pauses. "Hi, Rafe."

"Annika." He kisses her cheek, as well, but the look he gives her is anything but friendly.

It's intimate.

How did I miss *that*?

"Come on in, everyone. Dinner's almost ready. Ivie's checking on it right now."

"Ivie's here?" Shane asks, his interests piqued.

"I thought it would be fun if she joined," Annika replies as we all take seats around the large living room. The house is traditional, all of the rooms separate—no open-concept here.

But it's beautifully decorated, and I know that Annika invested a lot of time making this house a home for Richard and her.

"Where's your husband?" I ask, but before she can answer, the man does.

"Sorry, everyone," Rich says as he hurries into the room from the back patio. "I had to take a call."

Rich is tall, slender, and utterly *boring.*

I don't know what Annika sees in him. Sure, he's smart and comes from a good family, but he's as dry as a corpse that's been left out in the sun for a year.

I bet he only likes to fuck in the dark, under the covers, after a shower.

I wrinkle my nose at the thought and then smile when Rich turns his attention on me.

"Hello, Nadia."

"Hi, Rich. Thanks for having us over for dinner."

"Oh, it's our pleasure. Annika should get to see her family from time to time."

What the hell does that mean?

Before I can ask him, Ivie comes bustling out of the kitchen and almost falls on her face.

Poor Ivie. She's such a klutz.

"Whoa," she says with a laugh.

"Easy there." Shane immediately jumps up to help

her. He takes her hand, kisses it, and leads her over to the sofa.

"Oh, thanks. I'm good. Just clumsy. Annika and I decided to make lasagna with garlic bread and salad. It's just about done."

I notice Carmine and Rafe share a look.

There is so much happening here, all unspoken, and all I can do is watch in fascination. There's trouble in paradise with my cousin and her husband. Shane wants to get into Ivie's pants. And Rafe and Carmine clearly find it all comical.

This is the best entertainment I've had in years.

"I'm starved," Annika says with a grin. "Let's eat."

"Not too much pasta for you, darling," Rich says as he pats her shoulder. "Why don't you stick with the salad?"

"Why don't you let your wife eat whatever the fuck she wants since she's a grown woman and everything?" I turn to Rich with a toothy, humorless smile.

It's not returned.

And I give zero fucks.

He simply sits at the table, and we start passing around dishes, filling our plates as Annika pours the wine.

When she reaches Rafe's glass, he shakes his head, and she moves on to the next.

But the glare Rafe aims at Rich would make most men piss their pants.

"How are things at the clinic?" I ask Ivie.

"Great," she says with a nod. "We're busier than ever right now."

"What kind of clinic do you run?" Carmine asks.

"We have a medi-spa," she replies easily. "We offer services from simple facials to botox to reconstructive surgery."

"Plastic surgery?" Shane says.

"Sort of, yes," Ivie says.

"There's a lot of botox happening in this city," Annika says with a wink. "And thank goodness."

"I was thinking of coming in to see you," I say, pointing to the crows' feet around my eyes. "I have a few lines I'd like to take care of."

"You don't have wrinkles," Carmine says, staring down at me in surprise.

"Yeah, I do."

"I can fix you right up," Annika assures me. "And I'd love to spend some time with you."

"Can you fit her into your already busy schedule?" Rich asks, his voice hard.

What the fuck is up with him?

"I always have time for Nadia," she replies. Her voice is just as hard as her husband's. Rich's jaw clenches.

Yeah, I'd say the honeymoon is over there.

And I definitely need to talk to her. Soon. Find out what in the hell is going on. Annika has always been my best friend. My confidante. Sure, I've been busy since the wedding, but that's no excuse.

Whatever she's going through, she won't face it alone.

"Oh, my God, this is so good." I bite into a piece of hot, crusty bread. "Seriously, A, you're an amazing cook."

"Ivie and I did it together," she says with a smile and gazes longingly at the bread. "I'm glad you like it."

"Here, try it." I pass her the basket, and she shrugs, takes a piece, and then passes it back.

Rich isn't happy. The dick. And that only makes me want to offer her another chunk.

I *despise* men who try to control their wives like this.

Carmine and Rafe chat about stocks, and I tune them out because it's all Greek to me.

Shane flirts shamelessly with Ivie, making her blush like crazy, which I think is absolutely adorable. Ivie's shy, a little clumsy—or a lot, depending on the day—and while she's pretty, no one would call her a beauty queen. She's the perfect epitome of the girl next door.

But she's smart and funny, loyal, and also one of my best friends.

I turn my attention to Rich, who's shoveling food into his mouth and doing his best to ignore his wife, who I see is drinking wine like a fish.

And Annika doesn't drink.

I'm going to get to the bottom of this.

"I'm going to put more bread in the oven," she says

and stands from the table, pushing her way through the swinging door to the kitchen.

"I'll go see if she needs help," Rafe says and follows her.

Rich just rolls his eyes.

"I need to use the restroom. Is it just around the corner there, Rich?"

He nods and points to the hallway on the other side of the kitchen. There's another entrance to the kitchen on that side, so I stop and lean against the wall, just out of sight, listening to the conversation happening within.

"I've got this," Annika says.

"I can help. Jesus, A, what's wrong?"

"Nothing." I can picture the fake smile on her beautiful face. "Everything's great."

"Bullshit." Rafe lowers his voice now. "You look miserable."

"I—" There's no sound for a moment. "You shouldn't be in here."

"You never should have married that asshole," Rafe says. "You know it should have been me."

"And your father said no," she reminds him, and I stumble back in surprise. Annika wanted to marry Rafe Martinelli? Why would Carlo say no? Our families aren't enemies.

"Yeah, well, your uncle didn't like the idea, either."

Papa knew?

I scowl.

Why am I always the last to know about this stuff? And why didn't Annika confide in me?

I know it's not all about me, but it hurts my stupid feelings.

"Let's get this out to the table."

"Annika."

"Rafe, I can't do this. I'm a married woman whether I like it or not."

"And I'd say that you don't like it very much right now."

"That doesn't matter."

"Oh, yes, it does."

"I'm not talking about this anymore."

I walk around the corner in time to see Annika and Rafe coming out the other door, Rafe carrying the bread for the table.

I look at Rich. He doesn't even raise his eyes from his plate.

I feel like I've just entered an alternate universe.

"SHANE GOT IVIE'S NUMBER TONIGHT," I inform Carmine as he unlocks the door of the Airbnb.

"I saw," he says and shakes his head. "I don't get it."

"Get what?"

"Nothing."

"No, you started it. What, exactly, don't you get?"

"Look, if I answer you, I'm going to sound like a huge asshole."

I cross my arms over my chest, raise a brow, and wait.

Carmine sighs painfully, pushes his hand through his hair, and then shrugs. "Okay. I like her. She seems like a nice woman."

"But?"

"But she's just not Shane's type."

"And what type is that, exactly?"

"You know…"—he gestures to me, waving his hand up and down—"he usually goes for the supermodel types."

"You do realize that even supermodels don't look like that in real life, right?"

"You do," he says without even thinking twice, and I have to blink at him.

Then I laugh.

"No, I don't. I think you're a little biased. Which is sweet. Ivie's awesome. She's funny and smart. And, yes, she's pretty. Shane isn't good enough for *her*."

"I told you I'd sound like a jackass."

"Sometimes the person we fall in love with isn't what we expect."

"He's not in love with her."

"Not yet." I kick off my shoes and walk over to the freezer, grabbing a tub of ice cream. "Something else happened tonight."

"What's that?"

"Did you see how unhappy Annika looked?"

"I saw that she and Rich are most likely fighting," he says. "It doesn't take a professional to see that. He's a douche."

"He didn't used to be." I shove a spoonful of Chunky Monkey into my mouth. "When they were dating, he was sweet. Laid-back. Even a little bit beta."

"*Beta*? What the hell does that mean?"

"You know, not alpha. Not in your face, or the one to put his foot down about things."

"So…soft."

"A little."

"I'm no beta."

I laugh again and wipe ice cream off my chin. "No, you're alpha all the way. I don't like that things seem to be changing for her so soon after their wedding. She looked sad and *scared*."

"Do you think he hurts her?"

Carmine's eyes darken. I know this is a sore spot for him.

And it's something I respect.

"I don't know." It's an honest answer. "But you can bet that I'm going to ask her. I didn't like that he told her what she could and couldn't eat."

"I caught that," Carmine says. "And he didn't like your response."

"How many fucks do you think I give about that?"

"Less than none."

"You'd be right. Oh, and there was something else."

He opens his mouth for a bite of my ice cream.

"I listened in on a conversation between Annika and Rafe in the kitchen."

"Busy little thing, weren't you?"

I ignore that and keep talking. "Did you know that your brother and Annika had a thing going? That they wanted to marry, but our fathers wouldn't allow it?"

Carmine's face blanks in surprise, and then he blinks rapidly.

"No fucking way."

"I heard it with my own two ears."

"He would have told me."

"And I would have said that she would have told *me*. But here we are, neither of us in the loop, and I know what I heard in that kitchen. He said that it should have been him. And she reminded him that your father said no."

Carmine swears under his breath. "Jesus. Why didn't he say something?"

"I think it's time I catch up with Annika for lunch. Just us girls. We have a lot of talking to do."

CHAPTER 10

I'm loaded down with greasy burgers, fries, and shakes from another of my favorites here in Denver. Yes, I'm going to gain sixty-five pounds if I keep this up, but there's a method to my calorie-filled madness.

This is Annika's favorite meal in the whole world. And if I want to get information out of her, it won't hurt to feed her something extra delicious.

I walk into the medi-spa and smile at Ivie behind the front desk.

"Hey," she says with a bright smile. "You're right on time. The last patient just left, and Annika and I are officially free."

She clicks the mouse on the computer, then hurries over and locks the door.

"Annika is in her office, but we can have lunch in the conference room."

"Perfect. I brought a *ton* of food."

"You always were my favorite," Ivie says as she winks and knocks on Annika's door. "Nadia's here with food. Come join us."

"I'll be right there," Annika calls back.

"She's been in a mood today," Ivie says as she opens the door to the conference room. I set the bags of food on the table. "I've hardly seen her at all, and when I asked her what was going on, she blew me off. Very *not* like her. So, I'm glad you're here. Between the two of us, we'll get it out of her."

"I have plenty to get out of her," I reply and then sigh. "I hate feeling so disengaged from you guys. I miss you."

"You're here. We talk and hear from you. But we miss you, too. We need to be better about seeing each other more often."

"Agreed. I wonder what's going on with Annika." But I know. It's that asshole, Rich.

Ivie and I unpack the bags, and I just start to suck on the straw of my vanilla shake when Annika walks in.

I immediately know that something isn't right.

She doesn't look up as she sits in one of the comfortable chairs and starts unwrapping her burger.

"Thanks for lunch," she says.

"Look at me," I order her.

"Don't be silly—"

"Look at me, A."

She looks up, and I want to punch the wall. "What the hell happened?"

"What do you mean?"

Ivie leans in to examine Annika's face. "How did I miss it? Annika, you have a black eye. You tried to cover it up, but holy shit. What's going on?"

"Oh, it's nothing." Annika tries to laugh and pops a fry into her mouth. "I tripped while walking down the stairs, and—"

"No." My voice is hard and low and leaves no room for argument. "What. Happened. To you?"

With her eyes still trained on her fries, she shrugs a shoulder.

"I've been begging you to talk to me for days," Ivie says. Her voice shakes with emotion. "You can trust us. You know that."

"You're the only two I *can* trust," Annika whispers.

"Tell us the truth. Let us help." I reach over and take her hand in mine.

"I don't know who he is anymore," she begins. "As soon as we got married, everything changed. It was like a switch flipped, and he went from being a fun, laid-back man to the devil himself."

She rubs her forehead in agitation.

"Suddenly, he wants to control *everything*. Even what I eat. When he said last night that I should stick with salad, in front of all of you, I wanted the floor to open up and swallow me. I was *so* embarrassed."

"He said that you should get to see your family once in a while," I prompt her. "What was that about?"

"I've been telling him for weeks that I wanted to go see you or invite you here, and he kept telling me no. No way. He's systematically cut me off from my parents, from everyone I love—except for Ivie because we work together."

"Just let him try to cut me off from you," Ivie says with fire in her voice. "I'll cut his fucking balls off first."

"Down, girl." I smile at an irate Ivie. "Clearly, Rich can't get rid of us. We're here to stay. This all started after the wedding?"

"On the wedding night," she confirms. "We went to the honeymoon suite, and I took a bite of some cake—we had so much wedding cake left—and he took it away from me and tossed it in the trash. Said I'd never eat that garbage again. That I was too fat."

I've never experienced rage so swift and all-encompassing. I wish he was here right now so I could bloody his damn face.

"Since then, he's counted every calorie. I have to keep a log of what I eat and give it to him at the end of the day. If he thinks I'm lying, well..."

She stops talking, and Ivie and I share a look.

"He what, Annika?"

She simply points to her eye.

"He's been hitting you this whole time?" Ivie demands.

"Not often, but more than once is too many times."

"Why didn't you tell us?" I ask. "Why didn't you say something?"

"If I tell, the family will kill him."

"So?"

Annika shakes her head. "I don't want him *dead.* I just don't want him. But I'm married to him now. I'm just...stuck."

"Bullshit."

"No way."

Ivie and I speak in unison.

"Divorce *is* an option," I say. "My father will absolutely approve of that, especially when I tell him about the abuse."

"You can't." Annika grabs onto me, her movements desperate. "You can't tell. You have to promise me that you won't tell *anyone.*"

"Annika—"

"Promise," she continues. "I don't want them to hurt him."

"And why not?" I stand and pace the room, so frustrated that I don't know what to do with myself. "Annika, he's hurting you. Daily. Why shouldn't the family take care of it? Even if it's not death, he should be ostracized. He can go fend for himself. There's no place for him here."

"I agree," Ivie says. "You're not this woman. You're not a punching bag. No one is, and you have the resources to get out of this."

Annika sighs and rests her face in her hands.

"I can't leave him. Not yet."

"What else is happening that you're not telling us?"

"I think he's involved in something bad. I don't know what, but I have to keep an eye on him for a little while longer."

"To what end? I refuse to let you get killed over this, Annika." Ivie stands and leans over toward her friend. "You don't have anything to prove."

"I just need a little time," Annika insists.

I want to rail at her, and I can see that Ivie feels the same. But my cousin has dug her heels in.

"If he hits you again, you fucking call me." My voice is ice. "You call me, and I'll come get you."

"Okay."

I want to ask about Rafe. I want to convince her to leave that pitiful excuse for a man *today*.

But she's had enough.

Ivie and I share a long look. The silent message is clear.

We'll watch, and we'll protect her.

Two hours later, I can't get to Carmine fast enough. But on my way to the Marinelli office, I call my brother.

"Thought you didn't want my help," he says, and I roll my eyes.

"Don't be a baby. I have a question. When Annika

started dating Rich, and when he proposed, did the family do a standard background check on him?"

"Yeah, I ran it myself. He's so clean; he's boring. And his family is the same. Why?"

"I just left Annika."

I hesitate. I don't trust Alex with much, but he and Annika were close when we were younger. I think he'd want to know about this.

"Let's just say that Rich isn't the happy-go-lucky guy we all thought he was."

"What does that mean? Is he hurting her?"

I sigh. "I was at their house for dinner last night, and he was a major ass. The way he spoke to her, the way he looked at her, it was *not* good. And today, she had a black eye."

"What the fuck?"

"It just doesn't make any sense, so I wanted to reach out and ask if you'd run the background. I should have known that it was done, but I needed to double-check."

"If he's a con man, it slipped past me."

That wouldn't surprise me. Alex is lazy, and if Papa gave him the task of running the check, it wouldn't shock me if he just looked at the surface and then let it go.

Except this is *Annika.* And Alex has always had a soft spot for our cousin.

"What are you going to do now?" he asks.

"She asked me not to do anything for a little while, so I'll just be here in case she needs me."

That's not the whole truth, but he doesn't need to know the rest.

"Keep me posted, please," he says, his voice softening. "If this continues, we'll take care of it."

"Yeah. We will. Okay, I'll let you know if anything else happens."

He clicks off without saying goodbye, and I hurry into the office to see the three Martinelli brothers all huddled around computers.

They are a sight to behold. Carmine and Shane are both tall, dark, and handsome, with chocolate eyes. Rafe is on the lighter side with blue eyes, but there's no mistaking them for siblings. And just walking into this room would send a normal woman's blood pressure into the stroke-zone.

"I might have something," I say as I walk into the room. All three heads come up to look at me.

"Hello," Carmine says as he stands and pulls me to him for a kiss. Right there, in front of the others. "I haven't seen you all day."

"Don't get mushy in front of your brothers."

"I'll get mushy wherever I damn well please."

I laugh as Shane clears his throat.

"Stop pawing at her and let the woman talk."

"Yeah." I slap at Carmine's shoulder as I pull away. "Stop pawing at me."

"You didn't seem to mind last night."

"Really?" Rafe demands.

"Fine." Carmine lets me go, and I push my hair away from my face.

"Okay, so last night, something seemed very *off* with Annika."

"Clearly, she and the new husband are having issues," Shane says with a nod. "You could cut the tension with a fucking knife."

"Definitely," I agree. "And he just wasn't acting like himself. That jerk isn't the guy we all knew before the wedding."

My eyes are on Rafe as I speak. His face is rigid, and he clenches his jaw as I keep talking.

"So, today, I decided to go see her, take her lunch, and do some digging. After all, Annika and Ivie are my two closest friends in the world, and if Annika is hurting, I want to know why. And I want to make someone pay.

"When I got there, I discovered that she had a black eye."

"What the fuck?" Rafe asks as he comes out of his seat. "The bastard hit her?"

"Yeah." My voice quiets. "He did. And he's done more than that."

I relay what happened during my lunch with my friends. When I finish, all three men are pacing the office, each with mutiny written all over his handsome face.

"I'll fucking kill him with my bare hands," Rafe growls, but I shake my head.

"She wants time. And here's the part that doesn't add up, though I didn't say anything to her at the time. She thinks he's up to something."

"Up to what?" Carmine asks.

"She didn't say, but my alarm bells went off like crazy. I asked Alex if the family did a standard background check before the wedding, and he said that he did it. But my brother is lazy, and I know he didn't dive very deep. He couldn't have."

"I can go so deep, Richard will feel me in his kidneys," Shane says, reaching for the computer. His fingers fly over the keyboard. "Yeah, this first pass is pretty standard. Credit score is seven-fifty. No jail. Really nothing to report at all."

"That's too tidy," Rafe says, his face still set in hard lines. "That reeks of cover-up."

"Agreed. It would be easier if I had fingerprints."

"Be right back." I turn to leave, but Carmine stops me.

"You're not going by yourself."

"Well, then get a move on, and let's go. I'll call Annika from the car. She can meet us there. Let's nail this whole mess on this slimeball."

Carmine and I hurry to his rental. I barely have time to fasten my seatbelt before he's peeling out of the parking lot and merging onto the freeway.

"How could my family let this happen?" I wonder out loud. "How the fuck did Rich make his slimy way into my family and start killing people? And why would he do it at his own wedding?"

"Smoke and mirrors," Carmine says. "If it happened at the wedding, he'd be the last person anyone would look at. Son of a *bitch*."

"Why does a random doctor from Denver want to kill your father?" I wonder out loud. "It doesn't make any sense."

"Shane's still digging. I don't buy this whole boring suburban doctor bit. He's hiding something, and we'll find out what it is. In the meantime, we need to get those prints, and we need to make sure Annika is safe. I don't like her being there with him."

"I don't, either." I shake my head and watch the city zoom by. "It was all I could do not to kidnap her and make her come with me. I don't want that asshole anywhere near her, ever again."

I'm just about to call Annika when my phone rings in my hand. "Hey, I was just going to call you."

"I need you." Annika breathes hard in my ear. She sounds panicked.

"What's wrong?"

"I need you to come to my house."

"Carmine and I are headed there now. That's why I was going to call. Are you hurt?"

"No, but if he gets here before you, I will be. Hurry. Please, hurry."

She hangs up, and Carmine steps on the gas.

"You heard?"

"Yeah." The set of his mouth is grim. "I don't know what I expected when we came to Denver, but this isn't it."

"No. It's not."

I want to thank him. His family is under no obligation to help with this. But I've learned one thing in the months I've known him: Carmine is a man of honor.

All the Martinellis are.

They may be part of a mob family, but they do what's right. And my instincts weren't wrong when I decided to start trusting him.

He's become much more than just a job to me. There are feelings in play that I haven't taken the time to dissect, to just *be* with and figure out.

There just hasn't been time. I need to do some sorting, determine where my head and heart are.

But for now, it's enough to be able to depend on him—and to know that I'm safe.

Carmine drives through the open gates of Annika's drive, and when we pull up to the front door, he cuts the engine, and we're both out of the car like a shot.

Annika opens the door, her eyes wide in shock.

"What is it?"

"Oh, God."

CHAPTER 11

~CARMINE~

"I knew it," Annika says as we hurry into the house behind her. "I knew something was wrong. I just found this."

She practically runs into an office at the end of a long hallway as if she has to get there before whatever's in there disappears.

"Is he here?" Nadia asks.

"No." Annika's voice shakes as she points to a trunk on the floor next to her husband's desk. "Look in there. Rich always tells me to stay out of this trunk, that it's none of my fucking business what's in here."

"Lovely way to talk to your wife," I mutter as I open the lid and stare down at what must be a dozen sandwich bags full of pills, a bundle of hundred-dollar bills, and a piece of paper.

"It's an address," Annika says when I pick up the paper. I open it, and sure enough, it's an address.

449 Oak Ave. 4pm

"He's a fucking drug dealer." Annika sits on the arm of a sofa and stares blindly ahead. "He's dealing. I want no part of this. I've worked damn hard to stay *out* of the illegal scene, Nadia. You know I have."

"I know."

"Where is he?" I ask as I turn to look at the two women. "Where is he right now?"

"His office, I would guess," Annika replies. "And if you're going there, I'm going with you because I want to give him a piece of my damn mind."

RICHARD'S OFFICE is across town, so it takes us a good thirty minutes to get there.

I don't know what kind of pills are in those packages, but I have a feeling it's the same drug that killed Armando at the wedding. I took a bag and the computer mouse from the desk to give to Shane for prints.

The three of us march through the medical plaza and up a flight of stairs.

"His office isn't attached to the clinic," Annika says, pointing to a door next to the clinic. "He likes having a separate entrance."

"How convenient," I mutter and knock once before turning the knob. To my surprise, it isn't locked.

"Well, shit," Nadia murmurs as she holds Annika back. "No, baby. No, you don't want to see this."

"Yes, I do." Annika forces her way through, and all three of us stare at Richard, slumped over his desk, white foam coming from his mouth. "Oh, Jesus."

"Keep her back," I say to Nadia. She nods, and I step closer to the desk. More of the same pills are in piles on the top as if he'd been counting them out to go into bags. Could he have accidentally taken one and killed himself?

Or did he do it on purpose?

Without touching the body, I search the space. I see no note, and nothing seems out of place.

I reach into his pockets and find his phone and wallet.

"Do you know the code to the phone?" I ask Annika.

She just blinks, staring at her husband.

"Annika."

"No. He wouldn't tell me."

"Can I take it to Shane?"

I just keep adding things to my brother's to-do list.

"Yes. My God, he's dead."

"We're going to leave everything exactly as it is," I say and take her arms in my hands. "We're going to sneak out of here like we were never here, and then we're going to call the police."

"Carmine," Nadia says in surprise.

"I could call the cleanup crew, but if I do, he'll go missing. His family will look for him. If we call the police, it'll be wrapped up as a drug situation gone wrong, and Rich's family can bury him."

"And I can play the part of the devastated newly-wed," Annika says bitterly.

"It's your call," I tell her. "How do you want to play it? Either way, you have to lie."

"Call the cops. His family will know that he was a drug dealer and a piece of shit. And they can bury him. But I won't act the part of the devastated widow. He didn't earn that."

"Okay, let's go. When we get to your house, you can call the office and ask them to get Rich from his office."

She nods, and we leave the way we came.

"I HAVE prints and drugs for you." I toss both items on the desk as Shane looks up in surprise.

"Where'd you find drugs?"

I fill him in on everything that happened over the past few hours.

"So, the fucker's dead?" Shane shakes his head. "Well, without the prints, I can tell you that I found quite a bit that piece of garbage, Alex, missed. Rich never went to college. It was all a front. And he didn't work at that clinic. He rented the office next door and pretended to go there to *work* every day."

"Holy shit."

"I'm still digging into some stuff, but these prints

will help. If my suspicions are right, Rich was behind everything all along. He tried to kill Pop, he sent out the feelers to New York, and when that fell through, he had that kid killed."

"But why? It just doesn't make sense." I shake my head, perplexed. "Why start wars with the mafia when he just came into the family?"

"Good question. Maybe he thought he was proving his worth to Nadia's dad so he could start working more intensely for the family. Who knows? How's Annika holding up?"

"She's damn pissed off."

"Yeah, I would be, too."

"Nadia stayed at the office with her. The police are probably there by now."

My brother's brow lifts. "Police?"

I tell him the plan and remind him that we have a few contacts in the Denver PD to make things go down the way we want them to.

"Looks like we have our man," Shane says. "Right here in Denver, all this time."

"It's a hell of a thing," I agree. "I wish he'd been alive when I found him. I'd have liked to break his fingers and then shove a pill down his throat myself."

"Are you sure it was self-inflicted?"

I shrug. "My gut says so. I think he poisoned himself by accident because he was an arrogant idiot. He was counting pills on his desk. No gloves."

Shane clicks his tongue. "All he had to do was lick his finger or something, and it would all be over."

"My thoughts exactly."

"So, what now?"

I shake my head. "I'm not entirely sure. I still have questions. Why would he have Nadia attacked?"

"Because she was digging around, and he didn't want her finding him out."

"You're right. It makes sense."

"I'm still going to keep digging on him. I want to know more, but I have a few other jobs coming up, so it'll take some time."

"He's dead. I'd say there's no hurry. Where's Rocco?"

"He got called back to Seattle. He's probably in the air by now."

I nod. "Thank you. For all of your help. You didn't have to."

"It's what family does," he reminds me. "Now, I'm going to load up and get back to my place in the mountains. The city gives me hives."

I laugh as Shane closes his computer and shoves it into his bag. He's a recluse, through and through.

"I'll lock up behind you."

"Want me to call Pop?"

"Nah, I'll do that, too."

It's late when Nadia finally walks into the Airbnb. She texted a while ago to tell me she was on her way.

Just from her text alone, I could tell she was exhausted.

And sad for Annika.

Nadia may do her best to hide things behind her hard exterior, but she's full of love and compassion, especially for those she loves.

She shuts the door behind her, then turns. Her eyes widen as she takes in the room. I've lit several dozen candles, and I have food waiting in the oven. But first, I'm going to pamper her a bit.

"Follow me." I take her hand in mine and kiss it, then lead her back to the bathroom, where a hot bath waits for her.

"Roses in the bath?"

"That's right."

She doesn't say a word as I help her out of her black shirt and blue jeans. When she's naked, I keep her steady as she steps into the bath.

"I didn't even realize I needed this."

"I did." I kiss the top of her head and let her soak. The wine I bought—Nadia's favorite—is chilled and ready, so I pop the cork and fill a glass. "Sip this while you soak. Just sip it. I don't want you to get drunk on me."

"What did I do to deserve this five-star treatment?"

I squat next to her and tuck her short, blond hair behind her ear. "We've been so caught up in things since we got here that I haven't done enough things like this."

"Is this goodbye?"

The question is a whisper.

"What do you mean?"

"Now that we know who was behind the murder, there's no need to work together anymore."

I lick my lips and watch her face intently. "Is that what you want? To go our separate ways?"

"It's the way it is. We did our parts. It's done. Now, we move on."

I nod and stand, walking out of the bathroom. She didn't answer the question. She didn't say that parting is what she wants.

It's definitely *not* what I want.

I pull out the steaks, potatoes, and salad, get everything plated and ready to eat, then walk back in to check on Nadia.

She's not in the bath.

She's in the bedroom, packing her bag, wearing nothing but a robe.

Excellent.

"What are you doing?"

"Packing, obviously."

I nod once. "Why don't you eat before you do that? I have dinner ready."

"I'm not hungry."

"Just humor me."

I take her hand once more and tug her behind me to

the kitchen, where our food awaits. She sniffs and then softens.

"You know I can't resist steak."

"I know." I hold a chair for her, then sit next to her and start cutting into my ribeye. "How is Annika tonight?"

"She was sleeping when I left. We went through some things in Rich's office, but then the police came, and then his family. It was just a mess. I got everyone but Ivie out, fed her, and then poured her into bed. Ivie's staying the night with her."

"She'll have a rough few weeks, but then she'll be able to move on with her life."

"I know. How do you move on from that, though?" She takes a bite of salad, seeming to think it over. "She was convinced that she knew him, was head over heels in love with him, and it turns out he was scamming her the whole time. How do you ever let yourself trust again? Fall in love again?"

"I think it takes a lot of time and healing." I pass her a hot roll. "She may need some therapy. Does your family have access to a psychologist?"

"Yes, my father has one on staff. She'll have a lot of support and anything she might need available to her, of course. I just feel for her."

"You love her." I take her hand in mine and squeeze.

"Yeah, and I can count on one hand the number of people who mean something to me in this world, and she's in the top three."

"Who are the other two?"

She frowns, pulls her hand out of mine, and returns her attention to eating. "How are Shane and Rafe?"

"Shane's back at his place in the mountains, and Rocco was pulled to something in Seattle."

"I can't believe you guys still call him Rocco."

I shrug a shoulder, watching her eat. Her lean throat moves as she swallows her food, her eyes heavy with fatigue.

She's magnificent.

And after tonight, she'll know without a shadow of a doubt that I do *not* want to say goodbye.

"I'm thinking Paris," I say, earning a surprised glance.

"For what?"

"For our first stop." I eat some potatoes. "A week at the Ritz would be nice. And then I think we should spend another week in the south of France, on the beach. There's a lovely resort there that I'll arrange."

"Did you hit your head today?" she demands.

"Not to my knowledge, no."

She takes another bite of steak and watches me. "So, you're going to take a several-week vacation in Europe? Awesome. Have fun."

"Not me." I wipe my mouth on a napkin. "*We.*"

"Who's we?"

"You, my lovely Nadia. And me. Us."

"But I thought you said—"

"I didn't say anything. I asked you if it was what *you* wanted, and you didn't answer the damn question."

"Okay, fine. I don't want to say goodbye. Is that what you want to hear?"

"Yes, actually. It is."

"But I don't see an alternative. I live in Atlanta. You live in Seattle. We're not working together anymore."

"The last time I checked, we're both adults."

"You know that it doesn't matter for us. Our lives aren't ours, Carmine."

"Do you really think our fathers will lose their damn minds if we spend some time together on vacation? I think they have enough to worry about."

She doesn't respond to that.

"So, we'll spend some time in Paris, and then in Cannes. We'll shop, we'll eat, and we'll explore. And I'll make love to you day and night, damn it. I'm going to soak you into every pore of my body. When it's all over, you'll be sick of me."

"Doubtful," she whispers.

"Sweetheart, don't cry."

"I'm not crying. There's an onion in my salad."

I scoop her into my lap and kiss her softly. "Let's enjoy each other for a while. No pretenses, and no tracking down murdering assholes."

"I should stay here for a couple of days to make sure Annika's okay."

"Of course." I kiss her once more. "We'll stay here for as long as you need."

"Carmine."

"Hmm?" I kiss down her neck, unable to resist her.

"I'm not going to fall in love with you."

I can't help but smile against her skin. She's everything I've ever wanted. She's my match in every way. And my opposite.

"No, there will be none of that."

But there already is. And we both know it. We're just too fucking stubborn to admit it.

CHAPTER 12

"He's in the ground, and it's time to move on." Annika rakes her hand through her long, blond hair and blows out a shaky breath. She's sitting on the couch, her feet tucked under her, still in her black mourning dress.

Ivie sits next to me. Now that the guests have gone and it's just the three of us, we've kicked off our shoes.

"I didn't think his mom would ever leave," I say, staring down into my wine. "She just kept going room to room, loading up everything she could into her arms like she was on a game show or something."

"I don't even care." Annika turns tired eyes to me. "She can have it all."

"And she'll take it." Ivie's voice is heavy with bitterness. And I can't blame her. "She has no right to any of it. You're his wife."

"Do you think I want it?" Annika demands. "I

couldn't care less about the clock he bought in Germany or any of the other *fancy* knickknacks he had lying around. I'd just sell or donate it all anyway. There are some papers that I need to go through myself, and I have my things, of course, but I can't get out of here soon enough."

"Did you say that the realtor is coming tomorrow?"

Annika nods. "I don't know when I'll be able to put the house on the market, but as soon as the lawyer gives me the go-ahead, I'll list it and find something else."

"You should buy one of those fun little condos downtown," Ivie suggests. "Right in the heart of the hustle and bustle. You can shop, eat, go to shows or games."

"I don't even know if I want to stay in Denver," she admits softly.

"What about Seattle?" Annika's mouth firms at my suggestion. "It's a great city, and I'm sure the Martinellis would give you the green light to live there."

"No."

I sigh and tip back my head. I'm done beating around the bush on this one.

"What in the hell is up with you and Rafe?"

Annika blinks rapidly, and Ivie scowls, first at me and then at our friend.

"I don't know what you mean."

"Oh, yeah, you do. I overheard you two in the kitchen when we were all here for dinner."

"It's not polite to eavesdrop, you know."

"Yeah, well, I'm not sorry."

"Wait." Ivie shakes her head and sits forward. "I'm missing something. Annika had something going with *Rafe?*"

"It was years ago," Annika says with a sigh. "We were kids. We'd see each other at things like weddings and such, and we both went to college at Duke."

"Rafe went to college at Duke?" Ivie asks, clearly impressed. "Wow."

"There's chemistry there," Annika whispers. "And, yeah, we saw each other for a while. But you guys, we're in mob families. Opposing ones. My parents would have thrown a fit."

I frown, thinking it over. "We aren't exactly at war with the Martinellis."

"But we're not on the best of terms, either. The betrothal between Alex and Elena fell through, and then they assumed our family had killed theirs for years. All of that happened at the same time. So you can't tell me that they would have welcomed my affair with Rafe with open arms."

I nod and shrug a shoulder. "Okay, so the timing was bad. But we're on better terms now. And if Rafe's who you want, I think you could make that happen."

"I don't want Rafe or anyone else involved in the organization." Annika's voice is clipped. "I never have. I thought I'd found a nice, settled, professional, and we'd live a boring, happy life in the suburbs. Look where that got me."

"It makes sense that you're not exactly ready to get back on the horse, so to speak, right away," Ivie says. "There's no rush."

"I don't know how I can ever trust anyone again," Annika says. "And while I do trust Rafe, I know that he's not the one for me. Not for the long haul."

"Why didn't you tell me that you had a thing going with him?" I ask her.

"Honestly, it was kind of fun to have a secret fling with someone I shouldn't. It felt taboo and reckless. But then I fell in love with him." She whispers the last three words, and I can't help but cross to her and hold her hand.

What is it about the Martinelli brothers?

"But it was a long time ago, and my life has changed. And I still don't want to be involved in the family business. He's neck-deep in it. It wouldn't work."

"I understand what you mean."

"Now, you tell us about Carmine," Ivie says with a smile. "Come on, spill it."

I don't want to hold back, so I tell them everything, from my father asking me to keep an eye on Carmine, to him *finding* me at the resort in Miami, and everything that went down since then.

It just feels so damn good to tell someone I trust what's going on.

"And now he's going to take you to France?"

I nod, thinking it over. "I should talk to Papa before he goes back to Atlanta. Make sure he doesn't have a problem with it."

"How does it feel to be in love with Carmine?" Annika asks.

"I'm not in love with him." I shake my head and stand to pace. "I mean, I *like* him. We have a good time together. The sex is *crazy.* And over the past few months, I've grown to trust him—which surprised me the most."

"But you don't love him." Ivie's tongue is in her cheek, and I glare at her.

"No. I don't love him."

Even I hear the lie.

"We're enjoying each other."

"Enjoy away," Annika says. "You've earned it."

"Right. I discovered that your husband was a killer and a drug dealer. I don't feel like I've earned a posh European vacation."

"I discovered it," she reminds me. "It's not your fault that I fell in love with a liar. Now, you can stop babysitting me because I'm a damn strong woman who can figure this out. And I have Ivie here. Go have crazy amazing French sex."

I giggle. "Is French sex different from regular sex?"

"Go find out," Ivie says. "We've got things handled here. I'll keep Rich's mom under control."

"Oh." I turn to her and prop my hands on my hips. "Did Shane ever call you?"

"Yeah." A smile covers her pretty face. "We've talked a bit. All on the phone. He's…interesting. Intense. Sexy as all get-out."

"What is it about the Martinelli brothers?" I voice the question this time, and we all giggle. "They're too sexy for their own good."

"I'M GLAD I CAUGHT YOU." I walk into my father's office, shut the door, and walk around the desk to hug him. "How are you, Papa?"

"I'm always better when my daughter comes to see me." He grins and kisses my cheek. "What are you up to, little one?"

"I just wanted to talk to you before you went back to Atlanta." I sit on the desk next to him and let my feet dangle, the way I've done since I was a small girl. "I haven't spent much time with you in a while."

"You've been busy," he says, leaning back in his wide leather chair. "I hope you're planning to take some time off now."

"Actually, that's what I wanted to talk to you about." I clear my throat. "Carmine invited me to go to France with him for a couple of weeks."

Something sparks in my father's eyes, but then he blinks, and it's gone.

"And did you accept?"

"Yes, but I thought I should run it by you, in case it's something you'd rather I not do."

"You're an adult, Nadia. You can spend time with whomever you choose."

My eyes find his. "You know that isn't true."

Papa takes a long, deep breath. "It's true. There are men that I would not be okay with you spending time with. Like Billy Sergi."

"*I'd* not be okay if I spent time with him." I wrinkle my nose. "The little worm."

"I hope you enjoy yourselves," Papa says. "There's a restaurant on the Seine that I highly recommend."

"Thank you." I bend down and kiss his cheek again. "I miss you, Papa. When I get back, let's spend a weekend together."

"I'd love nothing more, little one. Be safe. Tell Carmine I'll break both his legs if even a hair is disturbed on my precious daughter's head."

I laugh, but I know the threat is real. "No need to be violent. I'd better go pack. I think we're leaving this evening."

"Nadia."

I turn back to him with raised brows. "Yes, Papa."

"I love you."

"I love you, too."

"I THINK THAT'S IT." I walk through the Airbnb, making sure that I didn't forget anything. "I brought more than I thought."

"We shopped in New York," Carmine reminds me as he sets our suitcases by the front door.

"Ah, yes, how could I forget New York?"

He catches my hand and pulls me against him, then nibbles the side of my mouth. I immediately turn to mushy goo.

This man is potent.

"We're trying to leave," I remind him. "Not get naked again."

"I'll get you naked on the plane."

He lets go, and I stare after him. "On the *plane?* But we won't be alone."

"Close enough. And I have a very discreet staff."

And with that, he walks out the door, pulling two of the suitcases behind him, a backpack slung over his broad shoulder.

It's unfair that simply toting luggage is sexy on this man.

I grab my smaller bag, my handbag, and one last roller suitcase and let the door close behind me.

Our time in Denver is over. Now, we're on to France.

Denver International Airport is quite far from the city, so I sit back, expecting at least a forty-five-minute drive, but the driver leaves the freeway sooner than expected and takes us to a smaller airfield closer to the city.

"This is easier," Carmine says simply. He's holding my hand, softly rubbing his thumb over my knuckles.

Now that our attention has turned from finding a killer to just enjoying each other, he's much more physically affectionate than he was. And that's saying something because Carmine's always been handsy.

Not that I'm complaining. A girl could do far worse than having Carmine Martinelli's hands on her.

I'm not typically an affectionate woman, but with Carmine, the rules seem to fly out the window.

"This plane is bigger." I glance at Carmine. "You have *two* private jets?"

"No." He leans over and kisses my nose. "We have two private jets and a helicopter. Rocco flies the 'copter. I usually prefer the smaller plane, but this one is more appropriate for trans-Atlantic travel."

"Oh, right. Yes, it's better for *trans-Atlantic travel.*" I press my lips together so I don't laugh. I love teasing him. "You're so fancy."

"And you've just earned your first spanking."

He doesn't even look at me. Doesn't smile. He just steps out of the car and offers me his hand.

I don't bother sputtering a protest.

The ground crew is already loading our luggage onto the plane. We're greeted at the top of the stairs by a man in his fifties, wearing a simple black suit and a red tie. His hair is silver, threaded through with just a few dark strands, and he has a bushy mustache over his top lip.

He looks like someone's grandfather.

"Good evening, Mr. Martinelli. Ms. Tarenkov. It's a pleasure to have you aboard tonight. Please, make yourselves comfortable."

"Thank you, Charles," Carmine says with a nod. "Please let the pilot know that we're ready whenever he's given the okay to take off."

"Of course, sir."

I smile at the polite Charles and follow Carmine down a short hallway to a lounge area on the plane. There are cream-colored leather couches, a faux fireplace with a television hung above it, and a wet bar.

"We'll spend most of the next nine hours or so in here, but there's a bedroom back there." He points and then leads me farther back on the plane to show me a small bedroom with a king-sized bed and little else. "In case you want to sleep. Or...other things."

"I liked the couches," I reply and turn on my heel to return to the lounge. I sit, fasten my seatbelt, and pull my iPad out of my bag.

Carmine sits across from me just as Charles returns with a tray in his hands.

"What can I get you to drink?"

"Just water for me," Carmine says.

"A Coke would be lovely."

Charles nods regally and turns to the wet bar to fetch us our drinks. Carmine holds my gaze with his as

Charles fills glasses, delivers them to us, and then walks back to the galley.

"I could have gotten this myself if I'd known it was right there."

"Charles enjoys his job," Carmine replies. "We have lots of food aboard, as well, and he'll serve us dinner. And breakfast in the morning."

"Just like first class."

"Admit it. This is much better than first class."

I smirk into my glass. "It's a small step up."

Carmine's brown eyes are full of humor when Charles returns with menus so we can choose our entrées for dinner, and then the plane begins to move.

Within just a few minutes, we're airborne.

Once we've reached cruising altitude, Carmine unclips his seatbelt and moves over next to me. But rather than kiss me, or hold me against him, he simply holds out his hand.

"Give me your foot."

"Which one?"

"You choose."

I raise my left foot, and he starts to knead my arch with his thumb. I moan and lean my head back, closing my eyes as I enjoy the best foot rub of my life.

"You're good with your hands."

"I'm good with a lot of things," he reminds me. "I plan to spend the next nine hours reminding you."

"I'm so glad I'm getting a refresher course." I snort. "I think I've forgotten everything."

"You're extra sassy tonight."

I don't lift my head off the seat, but I turn to look at him. "I'm sorry. I don't mean to be difficult."

"I'm not complaining. You were tense in Denver. Worried. And as soon as we got on this plane, it was as though a huge weight was lifted."

"That's how it felt." I sigh, letting the tension from the last couple of weeks go. "I'm glad it's over. Still, I hurt for Annika. But we had a great talk last night, and I know she's going to be okay."

"She's going to be amazing. And now it's time for you to rest, relax, and let me take care of you for a while."

"I'm perfectly capable—"

He covers my mouth with his, playfully at first, but then it turns intense, and all I can do is grip onto him and return the kiss.

Finally, he pulls away and kisses my chin lightly. "Just enjoy, Nadia. For once in your life, don't over-think it."

"You talked me into it."

CHAPTER 13

~CARMINE~

"*Y*ou could shop anywhere in Paris," I say to Nadia as she leads me down a little cobblestone street tucked back in a corner off the left bank of the Seine in Paris. "And this is where you want to go?"

"Yes." She tugs on my hand and smiles at me. We arrived in Paris yesterday morning and spent the day in our suite at the Ritz, sleeping and fucking, recovering from jet lag.

This morning, she was ready to explore the city.

After I had my way with her in the shower.

"There's a little shop tucked away back here," she says as we stroll along the uneven sidewalk. "And it's the best. Just wait until you see it."

There are many *little shops* along this street, all selling different things—clothes, jewelry, art. But the store she stops at has me scratching my head.

"This?"

"Yep." She climbs the three uneven steps and tries the knob, but it's locked. "Jean Luc must be on a break. Oh, there he is."

She grins as an older man with little hair, wrinkled, leathery skin, and what's left of a cigarette burning in his mouth walks up with a frown.

"I only come for you," he says gruffly.

They don't hug or even exchange pleasantries, but he unlocks the door, and Nadia steps inside with an excited flourish.

I'm even more confused when I follow her.

The store is no bigger than my bathroom at home, and every surface is covered with things. If I were a claustrophobic man, I'd turn around and leave.

But I'm far too fascinated to leave now.

"Oh, Jean Luc, you never disappoint."

The man simply sits on a stool behind a tiny glass counter and watches Nadia. "I have a new Chanel. Vintage from 1968."

"Let me see it."

He reaches under the counter, pulls the signature black bag out, tugs a handbag free, and sets it on the glass.

"Oh, she's pretty. And the leather has really stood up well."

"It was hardly used, in all these years," Jean Luc replies. "I know you're fond of Chanel."

"Who isn't?" She grins. "I'll be hitting up Angelina tomorrow."

"Such a tourist trap now." He clicks his tongue.

"Yes, but *she* went there. Every day," Nadia reminds him. "And I do enjoy that hot chocolate."

"Who does not enjoy a cup of *le chocolat chaud* now and again?" he says, and unless I'm seeing things, he actually smiles at her. "Eight thousand."

Nadia's brows climb. "That's a little steep."

I want to interject. Eight thousand euros for a *used* handbag?

Jean Luc shakes his head and gives her a morose look as if she's physically hurting him. "Seven, then."

"Five," she counters.

"Nadia, you pain me. You can't find vintage like this, in this condition. I could sell to many others for more than five."

"Then sell it to them." She shrugs a shoulder as if it makes no difference to her, and Jean Luc sighs heavily.

"Six, and no less."

"I can live with six." She nods happily. "Done. Now, do you have a black Hermes Kelly?"

Jean Luc's eyes narrow for a moment as if he's pondering the question, but something tells me the man knows exactly what he has.

"For you? I will show you this."

He walks to a cupboard and pulls out another handbag, setting it on the glass next to the Chanel. A black handbag with a top handle and a gold clasp.

"Oh, she's beautiful. What year?"

"2004," he says. "Also, never used. Sat on a closet shelf for years."

He pulls out a pair of gloves before opening the bag and then showing it off to Nadia.

I'm lost. Who is Kelly, and why does she have a handbag named after her? I start to ask when Jean Luc tells her the price.

My eyes widen at the five figures that just came out of his mouth.

But Nadia doesn't even blink as she looks it over.

"Not even a scratch on the hardware," she murmurs. Her hands lovingly caress the leather as if she's touching a lover.

As if she's touching *me.*

"Jean Luc, you just sold yourself a Kelly. I'll take both."

"I have new jewelry," he begins, but Nadia shakes her head with a laugh.

"I'm going to stop while I'm ahead. But thank you. And thank you for opening your shop just for me. On a *Tuesday* morning."

"The French don't keep American hours," he reminds her, but his eyes are full of humor. "Who is your man?"

"I'm sorry, I got so excited, I completely lost my manners. Jean Luc, this is Carmine."

I shake the other man's hand, surprised by his firm grip. "It's nice to meet you."

161

"And you. Coming to Paris to fall in love is always a good idea."

This makes Nadia blink rapidly and seems to catch her off guard.

"Paris is called the city of love for a reason, no?" he continues as he gets the two new purchases ready for Nadia to take with her. "I thought Nadia would never find her man, but I see I was wrong. You've been coming to see me for how long now? Six years?"

"About that," she says quietly, clearly uncomfortable, but I step forward and take her hand in mine, giving it a squeeze.

"Six years, she always comes alone. Such a beautiful woman. I think she should be with someone. Not me. I am too old. But someone."

He takes her credit card and expertly uses the new machine discreetly tucked to the side.

"So I'm happy you called and came in today and brought your Carmine." He passes the card back and asks her to sign the slip. "I will worry less."

"Jean Luc, you're the sweetest." Nadia leans over and kisses his cheek. "You don't have to worry about me. I'm perfectly fine."

With fondness, he tucks an extra little box into Nadia's bag and walks us to the door.

"Enjoy your time in Paris. You're welcome to come see me anytime."

"My credit card is already weeping," Nadia says

playfully. "But you know I'll come see you every time I'm here. Take care, Jean Luc."

He waves us off, and we stroll away. I take the bag to carry and lean over to kiss her temple.

"That made you uncomfortable."

"I've never known that man to talk so much," she says. "He's always so quiet. I assumed he didn't speak English well. Then, I bring you with me, and he's Chatty Charlie. It's just weird."

"No, weird is paying what you just did on used purses."

She gives me the side-eye and then raises her chin defiantly. "You just don't understand."

"Then explain it to me. I'd love to see what you do when you look at those bags."

"Okay." She nods and then offers me a grin. "I'm getting hungry. Let's go to Café Flore for lunch. We can chat about it there. It's not far."

"You've spent a lot of time in Paris," I comment as we make our way to the café.

"I wasn't lying when I told you that it's my favorite city. When I don't have anywhere to be, I come here. I roam the streets, wander the museums, you name it."

"And meet interesting Frenchmen who sell you old accessories."

She smirks as we cross the street to the café. We're seated, and to my utter shock, Nadia orders our lunch in perfect French.

"What?" she says when she turns back to me.

"You speak French?"

"Yeah, but don't tell Jean Luc. I like him thinking I don't so I can pretend not to understand when he tries to upsell me." She winks and takes a sip of her coffee, but her face sobers as I continue watching her. "What is it?"

"There are moments I realize that I don't know nearly enough about you." I reach over and take her hand. "I thought I'd already learned so much, but I realize that I've only scratched the surface with you, Nadia."

"Well, we spent the better part of three months lying to each other," she reminds me. "Then, we had a job to do."

"That's not a good excuse."

"It works both ways, you know. I don't know much about you, either."

"Then, for the next two weeks, we're going to do exactly that. Learn about each other. So, tell me about the bags."

She shimmies in her seat. "My favorite topic."

"What was it about these two bags that you loved?"

"It's two very different reasons. We'll start with the Chanel. Coco Chanel lived here in Paris, at the Ritz, actually, but she also had an apartment above her boutique. She didn't sleep there. She gave parties and worked there. I've never been upstairs, but I've been on *the* stairs, and it's a trip, let me tell you. Anyway, she went to a little café near the Louvre called Angelina.

Every single day. She sat at the same table and always ordered the hot chocolate. It's a short walk from the Ritz. We'll go. You'll never feel the same about hot chocolate again. And I think Chanel's quality is insanely good, especially the vintage pieces. And because this bag was made before her death, she may have held it herself. I love the history of it, and it's always in style."

"Fair enough. And the other?"

"That was Grace Kelly's favorite handbag. Hence the name, the Kelly."

"Ah, makes sense now."

She smiles and leans back as our lunch is served. Once the waiter bustles away, she eats a fry and then keeps talking.

"These bags are made by hand, here in France, by artisans. Each one takes a lot of hours to make…"

I sit and watch her perfect face as she talks, using her hands for emphasis, explaining in detail how every product makes its way to a storefront.

Her enthusiasm is contagious. I don't need a bag, but she has me ready to run out and buy the first one I see.

"And here I thought you were all about the family," I reply when her story winds down.

"I am." She takes a bite of her sandwich. "It's always the priority and will be until the day I die. But this is a fun hobby."

"An expensive one."

"Says the man who bought a ten-thousand-dollar watch in New York."

"It wasn't secondhand."

Her laughter is a drug.

"Have you spent much time in Paris?" she asks.

"Not as much as you," I reply. "And I've only really seen the most touristy of places."

"Then we'll avoid those." She chews thoughtfully. "Will you think I'm weird if I suggest a cemetery?"

"Are you planning to kill me, then?"

"No. I've heard about a really beautiful cemetery here in Paris. If you're up for it, we could go check it out this week. The weather's beautiful."

"I'm game."

"Bet you never thought you'd be hanging out with me in a cemetery, did you?"

"Honestly, I never thought I'd be with you at all." I push my finished plate aside.

"Same." She rests her chin in her hand. "I told my father about us coming here."

I raise a brow in surprise. "And what did he say?"

"He didn't seem to care in the least."

"And if he did?"

She sighs and glances down at her empty cup of coffee. "If he'd been angry or forbade it, I wouldn't be here." Her eyes find mine again, and I see the heaviness in them. "We have responsibilities, Carmine. To our fathers. I love him. I respect him. And, at the end of the day, I guess I'm trying to prove something to him. So, as much as I wish I could say that I'd tell him I'm a big girl who can call her own shots, I know that's not the case."

"I understand." It sits like a lead ball in my stomach, but I do understand. Because I'd do the same thing.

I, too, had a conversation with my father before we came to Paris. And if he'd been unhappy with it, well, I'd be in Seattle.

Alone.

"Do you ever wish we weren't...?" She waves her hand in the air, not finishing the sentence.

"Intelligent? Wonderful? Wealthy? Witty?"

"Part of the organization, you moron," she interrupts with a laugh. "And, I should add, modest."

"No." I reach for the check and put my credit card in the leather folder. "I don't wish that. Do you?"

"No. I'm not like Annika. She hates it. Wants to be as far removed from it as she can. But I always found it fascinating."

"Maybe it ties in with your love of history," I suggest, and she nods.

"I think so. Our family goes back generations. To Russia. I used to love sitting on my father's knee and listening to him tell stories from his childhood about his parents—and theirs. My family has been in our line of business for hundreds of years."

"That's something we have in common." I sign the check and reach for Nadia's bags. "Let's go back to the hotel."

"I could use a little rest."

WE'VE JUST REACHED our suite when I get a call from Rocco.

"Isn't it the middle of the night there?" I ask.

"Early morning," he replies. "Just giving you a heads-up. Someone broke into Gram's house last night."

I narrow my eyes and watch as Nadia sets her new bags in the closet, then starts taking her clothes off. "What the fuck?"

"What is it?" she asks, but I hold up my hand.

"The alarm went off at about two this morning," he continues. "Our security was there within ten minutes, and the cops came five minutes later. A window was broken. I don't know what they took. If anything. They didn't make much of a mess."

"I wonder if they were looking for something specific."

"If they were, they found it and bailed. No prints. They took out the cameras."

"Damn it."

"Yeah, I know. We're locking it down, and I'm going to live there for a while. It's not good that it's been sitting empty for this long. We need to sell it, Carmine."

"And do what with all of her shit?" I rub a hand over

my face. "I'll be home in a couple of weeks. Let me know if this happens again."

"Will do. Have a good vacation."

He clicks off, and I turn to find Nadia watching me with concern. "What happened?"

"My grandmother passed away last year."

"I remember. We went to the funeral."

I nod and recall seeing her at the church. "Her house has been sitting pretty much empty since she died. I went through a lot of stuff because I was trying to find Elena, which is another story. But aside from that, there's ten thousand square feet and sixty year's-worth of shit to sort through."

"And someone broke in."

"Yeah. We shouldn't have left it that long. Rocco's gonna stay there for a while."

"It was probably a professional. Someone who staked it out and knew that it was empty."

"Most likely," I agree and push my finger into the waistband of her jeans. "Now, let's forget about the goings-on more than an ocean away."

"What do you have in mind?"

CHAPTER 14

~NADIA~

"*I* want to be with you," he murmurs as those talented lips take a slow journey down my neck to my shoulder. His hands skim down my arms, over my naked torso, and down to my ass, still covered in denim.

He squeezes, and my core clenches in response. But before I can say anything, his hands grip my thighs, and he lifts me like I weigh nothing. I wrap my legs around his waist, and he carries me to the dining room table.

"I want to kiss you." He unfastens my jeans, and I lift my ass so he can guide them over my hips and down my legs.

The underwear follows, and I'm left lying naked and spread wide for him.

I expect him to dive right in, wrap his lips around me and take me for one hell of a ride.

But to my surprise, that's not what he does at all.

His fingertips barely brush my skin, sending goose-bumps all over me.

"You're so fucking soft," he whispers before kissing my inner thigh. "So damn responsive. God, you're getting wetter by the second."

"Come on, Carmine. You're killing me here."

He just shakes his head and continues taunting me, teasing me. His touch is gentle, his kisses wet and carefully placed over my already heated skin.

I arch my back, wanting nothing more than to have him fuck me hard on this table. What's with the gentle shit?

Sex is impatient. Fast and dirty.

It's not *this.*

"Carmine," I breathe when his fingers brush over my most intimate lips. "Jesus, don't be such a tease."

He chuckles and licks up my stomach to my navel and then farther to the underside of my small breasts.

Who knew that little spot was so damn sensitive?

"You're killing me."

"Just relax," he croons. His voice is thick and sounds like melted chocolate. Full of lazy lust and affection, and it does something to me.

Something I don't recognize—or particularly feel comfortable with.

My throat closes, and my core clenches when his lips drag up over one already perky nipple. I don't know what this is. My already raw emotions are even more on the surface, and I don't like it. I don't want to feel vulnerable with him.

"Damn it, Carmine, you're going too slow. Just fuck me already!"

He stills, pulls his hands back, and raises his head to look down at me. "That's not what I'm doing here, Nadia."

"What *are* you doing?"

My breasts rise and fall with my breaths, coming faster now. What is all of this *emotion*?

"I don't have to spell it out for you."

"Yeah, I think you do. You have me tied in knots here. Just *do* it already. What's wrong with you?"

His eyes narrow, and if I'm not mistaken, he looks hurt. But before I can say anything, he quickly unfastens his slacks and pushes into me, hard.

"Is this what you want?" he demands and then slams into me again. And again. "You just want me to fuck you?"

I grip onto the edge of the table and hold on tight, but he suddenly stops and swears under his breath.

"Goddamn it."

"Carmine."

"Just give me a second." He shakes his head, and I can see despair there. Confusion. So, I sit up and take his face in my hands. "A few months ago, I would have simply fucked you until you walked wrong and been content with that. But that's not where we are anymore, Nadia."

I frown as he kisses the palm of my hand. "Carmine, we're enjoying each other. Having a good time together."

"Yeah, we are, but it's more than that. And if you say it's not, that you don't have any feelings for me beyond that, you're lying."

I bite my lip and feel my eyes fill. And that just pisses me off.

"Don't cry, baby."

"I'm not." I clear my throat.

"I can't just fuck you and then go on with my day. Not anymore. I feel more than that, and I'll be damned if I continue denying it—if that's what you're asking me to do."

"I don't know what I'm asking."

"Why is this so hard for you?" He brushes his thumb over my lower lip, his eyes following the movement.

I *want* to give in to my feelings for him. I *want* to fall in love with him.

"Of course, I have feelings for you. Maybe tender sex just isn't my thing."

"You're not a great liar."

"I'm an amazing liar," I disagree and narrow my eyes. "But maybe I'm not lying about that."

"You are. Tell me why you don't want to be vulnerable with me like this. Jesus, Nadia, we've been honest with each other about so many things over the past few months. We've seen a lot and been through more. Why does this level of intimacy scare you?"

I shake my head. I don't want to admit that I'm scared, and I hate him for putting me in this position. Why can't we go back to it being simple?

Why do I find it so hard to do this?

"What if I get my heart set on something that isn't possible?"

There. I said it out loud.

The look in Carmine's brown eyes softens, and he tips his forehead against mine. "We don't know that it's impossible."

"We don't know that it's not," I say and hear the tremble in my voice. "Falling in love with you, *really* falling in love, was never part of the plan."

"No. It wasn't." He kisses me gently. "I hated your guts for a long, long time, Nadia. I wanted to make you hurt. Wanted to make your whole family pay."

I frown. "Well, that's one way to make me feel all warm and fuzzy."

"Smartass." He smiles and kisses my nose. "But then I spent time with you, learned who you are. And I know that not only are you not the one I should hate, but I respect the hell out of you. You're going to make one hell of a Bratva boss one day."

My mouth just opens and closes in surprise. I've never felt more naked. Exposed. Not just physically but emotionally, as well.

He's still inside me, and he just stripped my emotions bare.

"I want that," I whisper.

"I know. And you deserve it. But even more than that, I've grown quite fond of the woman you are. One who enjoys sweets and can kick ass. Who isn't afraid to ask for help when she needs it. A woman who spends more money than some people make in a year on a used handbag."

"You really need to get over that."

He laughs and finally starts to move, slowly, in and out of me.

"You're everything," he says. It sounds so simple but carries *so* much weight. And all I can do is show him how I feel because I can't say the words.

I just can't.

I brush my fingers through his hair and kiss his shoulder as he slowly makes love to me. And after I have the craziest climax of my life, he carries me to the bedroom.

"We aren't done yet."

"You may not be, pal, but I'm exhausted."

He chuckles and kisses my cheek. "We'll wake you up again."

OKAY, so there's something to be said for making love.

I've never done it before.

I feel energized the next morning. Satisfied. And oddly…sentimental.

I'm not an overly romantic girl. Damn him for

digging his way under my skin when I wasn't looking and making me get all used to him.

"Here we are," Carmine says as our taxi stops next to the entrance of the cemetery. He takes my hand, and we walk over to the towering iron gates.

"This place is huge," I say as I look at a map. "We might be here awhile."

"We have all day."

We walk inside, up a short hill, and then all I can do is stand and gape. The cemetery is enormous. The headstones are old and different, and I can't wait to check them all out.

"Let's go this way and then check out the mausoleums last," I suggest.

"Lead the way," he says, gesturing with his arm. He's dressed casually today in a black T-shirt and cargo shorts, and he makes my mouth water.

How can a man look like that in a shirt and have it be legal?

I have no idea.

I'm in a simple red sundress today because it's summer in Paris and it's warm. Thankfully, I also have a good-sized crossbody bag that holds my concealed carry, and I have a smaller piece tied to my thigh.

Yes, we're on vacation, but you can never be too careful. I saw Carmine slip his handgun into a holster in the waistband of his shorts, above his impressive ass.

"It just goes on and on," I say and point out a statue.

"That headstone looks like a woman weeping, and she's holding the hand of someone in a jail cell."

"This whole place is a work of art," he says.

"I hope this isn't boring for you."

"Not at all." He takes my hand in his and kisses my knuckles. "It's fascinating. And I'm with you. How could I be bored?"

"Good point." I wink at him and then glance over my shoulder. It looks like someone is watching us.

I do a double-take, and the person is gone.

Huh. I must just be on edge today. My emotions are all over the place, and I'm keyed up. That's all.

Nothing to worry about.

"Okay, this is…interesting." I stop next to a large concrete casket covered in moss. But coming out of the top are two arms with the hands touching, as if two people are buried here, holding hands even in death.

"I don't think I want to be buried like that," Carmine says thoughtfully.

"You don't think it's romantic?"

He glances down at me. "Do you?"

"I don't know. It's kind of macabre, but it's also kind of sweet."

We wander around some more and see the graves of Chopin, Oscar Wilde, and other artists. The memorials are absolutely stunning.

Then we turn a corner, and behind a chain-link fence is the grave of Jim Morrison.

"It's a shame they had to close it off because of vandals," I say. "But still cool to see."

"Do you like The Doors?"

"Sure." I shrug and glance back.

The same man is there again.

"I think—"

"Yep, I saw him. We'll find a more private spot and confront him."

I nod and, hand in hand, we walk down a road in the cemetery that looks as if it belongs in New Orleans with beautiful aboveground mausoleums.

"These are beautiful."

"It's amazing how different every part of the cemetery is."

"I agree."

I glance back but don't see the man following us any longer. But just as we turn a corner, he walks out from behind a crypt, a knife in his hand.

"Get in here," he hisses. "Now. Don't make a scene."

Carmine squeezes my hand, and we follow him into an open mausoleum. We slip inside, and he shuts the door.

"Who the hell are you?" Carmine asks, but the man strikes out with the knife, and I take out his knee.

He crumples to the ground, but he lashes out with the blade again.

Carmine punches him, then picks him up and holds him by the collar. "Who the fuck are you?"

"You're going to die today," the man growls, but

before he can wave the knife again, I bend his hand back and take it from him, then press my gun to his head.

"Answer the damn question."

His eyes jitter back and forth between Carmine and me.

"You're not exactly discreet," Carmine says, his voice perfectly calm but hard as stone. "Either you wanted us to see you, or you're shitty at this job."

"Fuck you."

"I don't think so." Carmine knees him in the stomach, sending him to the ground once more, wheezing. We circle him slowly.

"Who sent you?"

"I'm not telling you *shit*."

I smile sweetly and squat next to him. "Oh, yeah, you are. Because if you don't, you won't leave this place alive. You'll spend all of eternity here with the…"—I check the name on the crypt next to me —"the Bettencourts. I'm sure they're nice people. And there's plenty of room here for you. You like to snuggle with corpses, don't you? I mean, they've been here since…"

I recheck the tomb.

"Since 1928. They're probably nice and decayed by now."

He looks green; like he's about to throw up.

"I won't ask nicely again," Carmine says.

"Richard hired me to follow you," he snaps. "I've

179

been tailing you since you were in Denver. I'm just supposed to keep an eye on you and report back."

My gaze flies to Carmine's, and I stand to talk to him.

"How does he not know that Rich is dead?" I murmur.

Carmine shakes his head and then looks down at the man and curses. "Are you…"—he waves his hands around—"*crying?*"

The man is just sitting there, weeping.

"There's no crying in the mafia."

"Why are you quoting movie lines?"

He turns to me. "Because there's no crying. He's crying."

"Yes, I know."

We both turn back to him and swear.

"Fucking hell."

He's already seizing, foaming at the mouth. "He took a pill."

"He'd rather die than give information," Carmine agrees, and we watch until he stops jerking.

"What now? We can't leave him like this. Someone will find him. A groundskeeper or someone."

"We do what you suggested. Open that crypt and put him in there with the nice Battencourts."

I raise a brow. "Ew."

"I'll do it."

"No, I'll help." First, I poke my head out the door to

make sure we haven't drawn a crowd. That would be uncomfortable.

But no one is even about.

"It's clear."

Carmine nods and opens the tomb. We both look down at the man.

"Wow, he looks good for being dead for almost one hundred years."

"The embalming did its job," Carmine agrees. "Nice suit, too."

"Well, this is a nice mausoleum. They had money." We turn back to our stiff. Carmine grabs his shoulders, and I take his feet, and we maneuver him into the burial chamber. "He just fits."

"No one will find him for a long time." We close the lid and have to push down for it to settle. "If ever."

"I don't get it." I straighten my dress and return my gun to its leg holster. Carmine picks up the knife and wipes it free of prints, then opens the other crypt. I walk over to look. "His wife."

"She doesn't look as good as he does."

The skin on her face is mostly gone, leaving her teeth showing. I check the date.

"She's been dead twenty years longer. They didn't embalm then."

He tosses the knife in with her and closes the top.

"You know the most interesting things, sweetheart. You were saying?"

"I don't get it," I continue. "He didn't know that

Rich was dead. It wasn't a secret. You and I were at the funeral. If he was following us like he said, he would have seen us there."

"Maybe he was off work that day," Carmine says with a shrug and walks over to the door. "I don't really care. He's not following us now."

He opens the metal gate, and we step out, much to the surprise of a young couple currently walking around through the cemetery.

"Oops." I grin and wipe my mouth, then wink up at Carmine. "Finally checked that one off the bucket list."

Carmine laughs and pulls me away, just as the young woman gasps.

"Never a dull moment with you, is there?"

"Nope. And you're welcome."

CHAPTER 15

~CARMINE~

"You really should come in with me," Nadia says as she treads water in the crystal-blue pool. We've been at the resort in Cannes, on the French Riviera, for five days. We went from sightseeing and walking all over Paris to lazy days by the pool and eating all of the food in sight.

It's all about balance.

"I'm happy to sit here and watch," I reply. Nadia just shakes her head and starts swimming back and forth. We're not alone here at the pool since it's open to all resort visitors. But because it's the middle of the week, it's not overly crowded, either.

I'm sitting on a lounge chair, similar to the one that Nadia was sitting in that day that I found her in Miami all those months ago.

But so much has changed since then.

Finished with swimming, she moves over to the infinity wall and stares out at the water beyond.

The view here is stunning. We've spent quite a bit of time on the balcony of our penthouse suite, enjoying the sunsets.

It won't be long before we're back home, immersed in all of the responsibility that comes with our lives.

But for now, we're simply enjoying our vacation. Together.

I take a sip of the fruity drink that Nadia ordered for me and watch as the woman turns from her view and gives me a smile as she swims through the water.

Her eyes widen in surprise, and I lean forward, wondering if she needs my help.

"Oh, crap," she mutters, and as she walks up the steps and out of the pool, her bikini top is in her hands.

And her breasts are bare and on display.

"You'd best cover yourself."

"The damn clasp broke," she says. "And I liked this suit. Oh, well, I brought another one."

"Put something on, Nadia."

She looks up and frowns. "We're in *France*. Trust me, no one cares that I'm topless."

"I care."

She tips her head to the side. "Seriously, it's no big deal, Carmine."

"Put something on, or we'll go to the room."

She simply sits on the chair, leans back, and tips her

face up to the sun, her small breasts out for everyone to see.

"No."

I press my lips together in frustration. "Nadia."

"Carmine," she says lazily and reaches for her drink. "I'm a grown woman. It's not illegal to be topless poolside in France. So, I'm going to sit here. Topless."

"For fuck's sake." I grab her black cover-up, toss it over her, and lift her into my arms. I don't miss the man across the pool, watching us.

He'll be dealt with later.

"What in the hell are you doing?"

I don't answer. I simply carry her to the elevator, and when we reach the top floor, I stride into our room.

She's glaring at me now.

I couldn't care less.

"You're such a fucking caveman," she growls. "I didn't do anything wrong, Carmine."

"Stop talking." I set her on the floor and then pin her against the wall. I take her hands in mine and lift them over her head with one of mine. With the other, I worry a nipple between my fingers. "If you think I'll sit back and let you sit out there on display, for everyone to see, you're sorely mistaken."

"*Let* me—"

"I said, stop talking." I drag my nose over the shell of her ear, breathing her in. My fingers pinch the nipple, just a little harder. "This, right here, is mine. Only for *me* to see."

She whimpers when I move over to the other side and pay that nipple the same attention.

"No one gets the pleasure of seeing this but me."

"Caveman," she whispers, but I can tell the anger has left her, replaced by pure, unadulterated lust.

I make quick work of her bikini bottoms and my shorts, and with her hands still pinned over her head, I boost her up and slip right inside of her.

"This is what happens when you defy me, Nadia. You piss me off and make me want to claim what's mine."

"Oh, my God."

"Look at me."

With her blue eyes on fire and pinned to mine, I work her hard, making her come fast. With the second orgasm, I follow her over and lean my forehead against her shoulder as I release her hands, and she wraps her arms around my neck.

I can't breathe.

And I can't let her go.

"Jesus, you do shit to me," I mutter.

"Same." She swallows hard and looks at me as I pull my face back. "It really bothered you, I guess."

"I wasn't playing."

Her mouth quirks into a grin. "I can see that. Fine, I'll wear the suit. But I could say the same."

"I'd look awful in a bikini top."

She smirks. "Do you think I didn't see the waitress flirting with you when she delivered your drinks? Or how the other women watch you when you walk across the pool area, wearing nothing but your shorts?"

"And how do they look at me?"

"Like they want to eat you alive. And I can't blame them." Her hands glide down my chest. "You're a sexy man, Carmine. You have muscles for days. Combine that with this smooth olive skin and that sexy face of yours, and well, you turn heads."

"Thanks for feeding my ego."

"I'm not. It's just how it is. But I don't wrap you in a towel and pull you out of there."

"I didn't like it," I repeat. "And I won't apologize for it. If you want me to wear a T-shirt at the pool, I'll do that."

"Well, that makes me just sound dumb."

"No." I grin and kiss her chin, then set her on her feet. "It makes you sound possessive, and that doesn't bother me so much."

"I'm going back down." She pads over to the dresser and pulls out a clean swimsuit. When she's dressed, she turns back to me. "Are you going to join me?"

"Yes. Would a tank top be too revealing?"

She laughs now and shakes her head. "You don't have to wear anything."

I slip the tank over my head and shrug. "If it makes you more comfortable, it doesn't bother me."

"We're sappy. You know that, right?"

"Darling, what a sweet thing to say."

THE CASINO IS loud and bustling around me. I'm seated at a high-roller blackjack table, sipping whiskey and watching Nadia from several yards away.

She's at a poker table, pouting because she just lost five thousand dollars.

"Well, poo," she huffs and gives the man beside her a forlorn look. "I'm really bad at this, aren't I?"

I ask the dealer to hit me and hold at nineteen.

"I've seen worse," her companion says. "Let's try this, shall we?"

His hand is on the small of her back and drifts down to her ass as he leans in to help her with her next hand.

My stomach twists.

He's going to lose that hand. And I'm not talking about the cards.

I win at nineteen and rake in twenty grand in chips as the asshole laughs and nuzzles Nadia's nose.

I sip my whiskey and act disinterested.

She loses again.

"That wasn't quite as bad," he tells her and moves in closer. "Now, for this hand, we'll do things a little differently."

I'm dealt a four of clubs and a queen of hearts. I tell the dealer to hit me and draw the six of diamonds.

I hold, and the dealer goes down the line of other players.

Nadia wins her hand and claps her hands joyfully, then kisses the man on the cheek.

That earns her ass a nice squeeze.

Fucking hell, how long do I have to watch this shit?

Finally, she whispers in his ear, and he rewards her with a wide smile and a nod of acceptance.

They leave the poker table.

I fold my cards, take my chips, and follow them.

"Are you on a good floor?" she asks, loud enough for me to hear her.

"The twelfth is nice and quiet," he assures her as they get into an elevator.

I take a different one and count my lucky stars when I get off just after them and follow them down the hall. He opens their door, and I hurry up, then push my way inside before he can shut it behind them.

"Hey, what's the big deal?"

"We could ask you the same thing," Nadia says, not smiling and flirting now.

He tries to act as if he doesn't know what she's talking about, but the longer we just stare at him, our weapons drawn, he loses the fight. He finally blows out a breath and holds up his hands in surrender.

"I guess you caught me."

"You've been following us for days," I reply. "And you're not very good at it. Just like your associate in Paris. Who's dead, by the way."

He narrows his eyes and then shrugs a shoulder. "He was a shitty operative."

"So are you."

This gets his temper up. "No. I'm not."

"We saw you," I repeat. "And what was that show downstairs? Did you think you could just flirt with her, and she'd jump right into bed with you?"

"And why not?" he asks, his voice bold. "We've all heard the stories about Nadia Tarenkov, fucking anyone who offers."

Without hesitation, I hit him across the face with the butt of my sidearm, drawing blood.

"Wait. Are you *in love* with her?" He laughs and doesn't bother to wipe at the blood on his face. "That's not even funny. It's sad. Pathetic, really. She'll just double-cross you, man. That's what she does."

"Shut the fuck up." Nadia kicks over the desk chair and forces him down into it, and I pull the twine out of my pocket and secure his hands behind his back.

"Why are you following us?" Nadia asks him.

"I don't have to tell you shit. Go ahead and kill me. You're going to anyway."

He's not wrong.

"Rich has been dead for weeks. Why are you still doing his bidding?" I ask.

He scoffs. "You think this came from *Richard*? Come on, Carmine, you weren't born last night. Pull your dick out of your brain and think about it. This comes from way higher up than Richard. That dude was a piece of shit. A total pussy."

"You know, I don't disagree with you," Nadia says as she walks around him. "But I never understood why men like to compare weakness to female genitalia."

She reaches down and grips his dick in a firm fist, making him yell in rage.

"When it's your *dick* that's so weak. So, the truth is, Richard was a dick."

Then she looks up at me and laughs. "Dick is short for Richard."

"Makes perfect sense, then," I agree.

She lets him go and walks over to me, urging me to the side so she can speak to me privately.

"Could it be true that Richard was working for someone else?"

"It could be, but Shane dug around on him and didn't find anything. He was going to keep delving into it in his free time. I'll have to call him and see if he found anything new."

"Yeah, let's do that. Ah!"

The asshole has Nadia pinned to the wall, his hands around her neck in a flash. I have no idea how he got out of the restraints.

"Let her go." I press the business end of my sidearm against the side of his head, but he doesn't let up on his grip. Nadia's face is already turning purple. "I said, fucking let her go."

No response.

I glance at Nadia and see that she won't last much longer.

So I squeeze the trigger and kill the son of a bitch.

"Jesus," she wheezes as he slumps to the floor, and she can breathe again. "Fuck."

"Hey, look at me."

She does as I ask. Her eyes are red. Her throat will be bruised.

I aim and shoot him once again.

"He's dead, Carmine."

"I thought he'd let go when I had the gun to his head."

"He was cocky and arrogant," she says when she finally catches her breath. She pulls an unopened bottle of water out of the fridge, but I shake my head no.

"Don't drink that. We don't know that he didn't poison everything in here."

"You're right. Christ." She drops the bottle to the carpet. "Who's going to clean up this mess?"

My smile is humorless as I pull my phone out of my pocket and tap a series of numbers, then send the text through.

"It'll be handled."

She just stares at me. "In *France*?"

"Anywhere." My answer is simple. "Your family would do the same."

She nods and pushes her hand through her hair. "You're right. I'm just rattled. I'm not used to being choked out like that. I guess it's safe to say that breath-play isn't my jam."

"No." I lean in and press a kiss to her neck where the bruises are already starting to form. "We won't be exploring that. There are too many other ways to bring pleasure. Let's go."

I don't spare the goon on the floor a glance as I open the door and lead her out, keeping an eye on our surroundings in case there's someone else lying in wait.

But as we leave the casino, we're alone. Once in the car on the way to the hotel, she leans her head on my shoulder.

"We need to go home," she murmurs.

"Agreed." I kiss the top of her head. "Vacation is over. We'll fly out tonight."

"Good. Are we going to Seattle?"

"Yes. Unless there was somewhere else you wanted to go?"

"No, Seattle works. I'll need to call my father when we land. I need to fill him in on what's going on."

"I think we should have a meeting with both of our fathers. Do you think yours would come to Seattle?"

She thinks it over. "If your father sends the invitation, I'm sure he will."

"I'll get that ball rolling. We thought what was happening in Denver died with Richard."

"We were wrong." She yawns. "We were very wrong."

And I'm furious.

No one will ever touch her like that again.

"I shouldn't have paused in shooting him," I say when we're in the elevator headed up to our room. "I hate myself for it."

"He might have stopped," she says. "Hey. I'm here, and I'm fine. We're going to figure out who's behind this, and we're going to kill *them*. No hesitation. No second chances."

"No. No hesitation." I pull her to me when we close the door to our suite and hold her close. We're rocking back and forth, clinging to each other, when my phone rings.

I don't let her go as I bring it to my ear. "Yes."

"The plane will be ready within the hour."

"Excellent."

I click off and tip her chin up with my finger.

"Let's go home, babe."

CHAPTER 16

~NADIA~

"That's your grandmother's house?"

Carmine cuts the car's engine, and we sit in silence, staring at the enormous brownstone home just outside of Seattle, still perfectly manicured and maintained.

"It is." He sighs and then turns to me. "My brothers, Elena, and I practically grew up here. Especially in the summers. The house sits on roughly twenty acres of land. More than sixty years ago, when my grandfather bought the property, he got it for a steal."

I raise a brow, and he laughs.

"No, he didn't *steal* it. But he got a great deal on it. Today, it's worth well into the eight figures."

"I bet someone would love to buy it, divvy up the land into smaller parcels, build, and sell. Make it a nice little neighborhood near the water."

"I'm sure they would. And they'd make a good deal of money off it. But that's not going to happen."

"So, you're just hanging onto it for what? Sentimental value?" I shake my head and get out of the car. "Carmine, this property is prime real estate to make your family money."

"We have plenty of money," he reminds me. "And we're making more every day. Now, let's go find Rocco and see what's going on."

He slips his hand into mine and leads me through an arched, double door entrance and into a grand foyer with a split staircase.

It's a stunningly beautiful home. And it suits what I know of Carmine's grandmother, the matriarch of their mafioso family.

"He's probably in the kitchen," Carmine says and leads me through rooms full of old furniture, artwork, and windows that offer a view of the water.

"I see why you have a thing for beautiful views."

He smiles. "I learned from her."

We walk past a dining room and into the kitchen, where sure enough, Rafe leans on the counter, tapping keys on his laptop as he munches on a sandwich.

"Hey," he says and looks up at us. "Jesus, you look like shit. Aren't you supposed to come home from vacation looking all bright-eyed and bushy-tailed?"

"What the fuck does that even mean?" Carmine asks with a laugh. "We came straight here from the airport."

"Ah. Jet lag. So, I hear you had some fun being tailed over there."

"You heard right," I reply and open the fridge, starving. "You have cream cheese. Do you have bagels?"

"Sure. Here you go."

He opens a cupboard, and I have my pick of everything, cheese, or plain.

I always go for the cheese.

"Want one?" I ask Carmine.

"Sure. I'll do it. You're exhausted. Here." He takes over, and I point to the cheese, then settle back to chat with Rafe.

"And you had a break-in here," I reply, to which Rafe nods.

"Yeah. Fucker got inside by breaking one of the big picture windows in the library. I had them repaired yesterday."

"But not with the original glass," Carmine says with frustration.

"No," Rafe agrees, then turns to me to explain. "Ninety percent of the glass in this house is original. It was built in 1909. Gram was particularly fond of the glass."

"I'm sorry. That sucks. What did they take?"

"As far as we can tell, nothing." He blows out a disgusted breath and paces the kitchen. "I've been through every room. Aside from the window, *nothing* was moved. It doesn't make any sense."

"Unless they were looking for something or *someone*

197

who wasn't here," Carmine replies as he sets a plate full of bagel goodness in front of me and then sits next to me with a plate of his own.

"I thought of that," Rafe says. "Since it's not been a secret that the house has been empty, I'd say it was some*thing* they were looking for."

"If it was a run-of-the-mill thief," I say, licking cream cheese off my finger. "He could have been looking for jewelry, artwork, antiques. But I saw a lot of priceless art and antiques on our way through when we arrived."

"And nothing is missing," Rafe says. "Father took all of the jewelry and any money Gram had lying around here home with him a few days after she died."

"So, someone broke in and was disappointed at the lack of loot," Carmine says with a shrug. "We'll ramp up the security, especially if you don't want to keep living out here."

"I don't really mind it," Rafe says, thinking it over. "It's just so damn far out of the city. By the way, I checked your house the other day. Nothing's going on there."

"We'll head over after we finish here," Carmine says. "But thanks for checking. I have around-the-clock security."

I finish my bagel and sigh in happiness. "Thanks for the carbs."

"You're welcome. Have you heard from Annika?"

I wondered if he'd bring up my cousin. Part of me wanted him to so I could drill him.

But the man standing across from me just looks...miserable.

"Yeah, we text just about every day."

"How is she?"

I tip my head to the side. "Why don't you ask her?"

"I have. She doesn't fucking reply." He drags his hands over his face in agitation. "She's cut me out entirely, and it's more frustrating than I can tell you."

"She's getting by," is all I say, but when he just stares at me, I continue, carefully choosing my words. "She feels foolish. And she's mad."

Rafe nods, and Carmine reaches over to squeeze my hand.

"If you talk to her, just tell her to text me back."

I laugh and then shrug when Rafe sends me a look that's likely made plenty of men piss their pants.

"I'll mention it. But Annika is her own woman, Rafe. And she wants *nothing* to do with the mafia. She's never made that a secret."

"I can't be held responsible for the family I was born into." The frustration rolls over his face as he shakes his head. "And neither can she. She has to stop punishing us both for it."

"Is that what she's doing?" I wonder. "Or is she simply trying to live a simple life?"

"She's stubborn as hell, that's what she is," Rafe says.

"On that, we can agree. I'll pass along your

message." I turn to Carmine, who's remained quiet as he listened to the exchange between Rafe and me. "What time are we meeting with our dads?"

He checks the time and then stands. "In a few hours."

"You're meeting with Pop *and* Igor?" Rafe asks with surprise.

"Yes. We need to talk about the men who followed us in France," Carmine says. "And I want to do it in a secure place. Over the phone or internet won't cut it. You're welcome to join us. Is Shane still in Colorado?"

"I'm not sure where he is," Rafe says. "He said something about a job in Colombia."

I raise a brow. "What, exactly, does Shane do for a living?"

"That, we can't tell you," Carmine says but takes the sting out of the statement with a kiss to my head. "Let's go home and freshen up for our meeting. Rocco, we're meeting at three, at the downtown building."

"In the office?" he asks.

Carmine nods and sets our dishes in the dishwasher, then leads me out of the kitchen and toward the front door.

I want to ask for a tour of the magnificent house, but I know that we don't have time. And, at the end of the day, no matter how close Carmine and I have gotten, I'm still a member of the Tarenkov family. There will always be a line. And taking me on a tour of the Martinelli matriarch's house might be crossing it.

We're quiet in the car. So much so that I close my eyes and rest. Neither of us slept on the flight here. We even went and laid on the bed, snuggled up, but couldn't doze off.

We didn't talk, simply lay there. Restless. Uncertain. Pissed off.

Someone's still after us, and we don't know who. Not to mention, I didn't like leaving bodies behind in Europe. It was supposed to be a *vacation.* We weren't supposed to have to kill anyone or constantly look over our shoulders.

Not that the looking behind you ever entirely goes away, even when you feel absolutely safe.

Because the truth is, being in the mafia means you're *never* truly safe.

I open my eyes when Carmine stops the car and then frown.

"We're not going to the penthouse?"

"No," he says and turns to me. "I want you here. In my home."

"I don't understand."

"When I first brought you to Seattle months ago, I didn't want you here because I didn't trust you. And I was with you for other reasons. It was all a farce. The penthouse was neutral territory, so to speak. But that's all changed."

He takes my hand and threads his fingers through mine.

"I want you here, in my house. Not the penthouse."

"But all of my things—"

"Have been moved here," he finishes with a small smile. "Come on, let me show you."

He hurries out of the car, then comes to the passenger side and opens my door.

"You were here once," he says as he pulls me up out of the car and leads me to the door. "And I certainly didn't trust you then, either. It irritated the hell out of me that you found me here."

"Oh, that was certainly the point," I reply with a laugh. "I wanted to frustrate you that day."

"You succeeded. But today, I'm inviting you."

"So, this is your home. And I see that it's not far from your grandmother's."

"No." He unlocks and pushes open the door and then leads me inside. "I loved spending time with her there. And I came to learn that I liked keeping my personal time separate from work. I like our building downtown, don't get me wrong. But it's not home."

I take in the expansive living space with new eyes. The style is *very* different from the home we just left, but it's no less opulent or beautiful.

"The kitchen is gorgeous," I say as we walk through it. "I enjoyed going through your fridge while you fumed."

He chuckles and leads me past, showing me guest rooms, a workout space, an office, and finally, his master bedroom.

It's big, but he's a big man, so it suits him. "More

views," I muse and walk to the door that leads out to a patio and a lush garden.

The master bathroom and drool-worthy walk-in closet are nothing less than what I'd expect of a man like Carmine, someone who definitely enjoys all of the finer things in life. It doesn't escape me that all of my clothes and personal things are in the closet, hung neatly.

"You have a lovely home," I say as he pulls me to him. My voice is sincere. It *is* lovely. "And it suits you."

"Thank you."

"You weren't kidding. All of my things are in that sexy-as-fuck closet. My shampoo is even in the shower."

"We won't be living at the penthouse," he confirms. "I hope that doesn't upset you."

Upset me? No. But I'd be lying if I said I wasn't a little confused as to where this was going.

Then again, maybe I'm just overthinking things. It doesn't have to *go* anywhere.

He kisses me, long and slow, as we stand in the middle of his bedroom. "We have time for a nap."

I smile at the suggestion. "Do we have time for more than a nap?"

His brown eyes narrow with lusty mischief. "Oh, yeah. We can manage that."

THE DRIVE into the city doesn't take long. With an hour of sleep and a round of lazy sex behind us, I feel surprisingly rejuvenated.

And I'm excited to see my father.

I've been in constant contact with him since the incident at the casino in Cannes. He accepted Carlo's invitation to meet in Seattle—much to my surprise and delight.

Carmine parks in the underground lot of his building. Rather than hitting the button for the penthouse in the elevator, he pushes the one for the tenth floor.

I raise a brow.

"This is the office."

"Your father's office?"

"No." He shakes his head. "That's on the twentieth floor. Don't worry, you'll see. It's more comfortable. Less imposing."

When we arrive at what used to be a condo but is now a beautiful office space, I see that he's right.

Rather than a large desk where an authority figure might sit, there are sofas, tables, and workspaces throughout. Someone stocked the kitchen with everything a person could ever need or want.

The decorations, in muted colors, are perfect for making someone feel comfortable and at ease.

Less than a minute after we arrive, Carlo walks in with Rafe right behind him.

His face lifts into a smile as he shakes Carmine's

hand. "Welcome home, son. Hello, Nadia. You look lovely."

"Thank you."

"Of course, she does. She's the spitting image of her mother," my papa says from the doorway. "Hello, little one."

"Papa!" I run over and kiss him on the cheek, then take his hand and lead him into the room. "I'm so happy to see you. Thank you for coming all this way."

"For you, I would fly to the end of the world." He cups my face and gives me a wink, then turns to Carlo and his sons. "Hello, my friend. Thank you for inviting me into your city."

"Thank you for coming," Carlo says as the two men shake hands. "My son made it clear that what he and Nadia have to tell us is very important."

"It is," I assure them both as we all take seats. I glance at Carmine, giving him a silent nod to go ahead.

"As you all know, Nadia and I were vacationing in Europe. A little holiday after discovering that Richard was responsible for killing Armando and several others. We thought the situation was settled with Rich's death."

He glances at me, and I pick up the story.

"However, while we were in Paris and strolling through a cemetery, we discovered we were being followed."

I recount the incident with the man in the mausoleum and how we handled it.

Carlo laughs, much to my surprise.

"I apologize. I know it's not a funny situation, but you hid the body in a crypt? That's just priceless."

My father chuckles with him, and I continue.

"A couple of days later, we moved on to Cannes, and within about forty-eight hours, we picked up on another tail. He was at the pool when we were there. At the same restaurants as ours. You get the idea."

I glance at Carmine, and he continues.

"We devised a scheme to catch him. And we did. But this time, when we told him that Rich was dead and asked why he was following us, he said that Rich wasn't the one who gave the orders. That it went *much higher than that.*"

Papa and Carlo share a glance.

"Do you know what that means?" I ask.

"It means this goes deeper than we thought," Papa says with a long sigh. "And someone tried to kill my daughter. Whoever is behind this will die."

"Who was Rich working for?" Carlo wonders aloud.

"We're going to fucking find out," Rafe says.

CHAPTER 17

~CARMINE~

"*F*or a doctor, your husband sure kept a lot of files at home," Nadia says to Annika. We're in Annika's home, in various areas of Rich's old office, poring over paperwork. He had tons of files, and every piece of paper has to be looked at.

"He wasn't a fucking doctor," Annika snaps back. She's sitting cross-legged on the couch, her dead husband's laptop in front of her as she tries to break the passcode. She sighs and leans her head back on the sofa. "Sorry. I don't mean to sound like a bitch. I wish I could figure out this password."

"For *not* a doctor, there sure are a lot of patient notes here," I muse as I open another file and frown down at medical information on someone named Samantha Briggs. "I would think it's illegal to have patient information at home."

"It is," Annika assures me. "It's also illegal to pose as

a doctor when you aren't. I'm so fucking mad at him." She stands and paces the office. "I wish he was alive so I could punch him in that smug face and then kill him myself."

"While I understand—and agree with—the sentiment," Nadia says, "that won't help us today."

"I don't even know what we're looking for," I reply and toss a file on the growing stack.

"Sorry I'm late," Ivie says as she hurries into the office, then promptly stubs her toe on the doorjamb. "Ouch! Son of a bitch."

"I swear, you need to wear Bubble Wrap," Nadia says, shaking her head. "Are you okay?"

"Yeah. That hurt." Ivie sits and rubs her toes. "I tried to get here sooner, but traffic was a bitch. So, how can I help? What can I do? Annika filled me in on the whole mystery at hand."

I turn to Annika and raise a brow, but the woman only shrugs. "She's my best friend, Carmine."

"I'm totally trustworthy," Ivie assures me. "I can help you look through the house or something, but I likely won't know what I'm looking for."

"That makes four of us," Nadia says. "None of us knows what we're looking for, but we'll know it when we see it."

"Something out of the ordinary," I reply. "Names, numbers, notes that are vague or even incriminating. That would be convenient."

"I'm trying to get into his computer, but the fucker locked it down pretty solid," Annika adds.

"How about this?" Ivie says. "I'll make you all a late lunch and help out wherever I can."

"I need a break from this," Annika says and tosses the computer onto the cushion beside her. "I'll help you, Ivie. We'll be back in a few with sustenance. Maybe I'll be more productive if I'm not hangry."

The two women leave the room, arm in arm, and Nadia sighs across from me.

"I guess it's a good sign that she's hungry," she says, still staring at the doorway. "She looks a little better than she did when we left here a few weeks ago."

I want to disagree. I think Annika looks horrible. The anger and hatred are festering inside of her. She has dark circles under her eyes, and she's lost a lot of weight in a very short time.

But I don't say any of that because Nadia is worried enough, and we have plenty on our plates.

"Carmine."

"Yes, sweetheart?"

"We're not going to find anything in these medical records. I don't even know why he has them here or what he used them for. But this isn't the answer."

"I agree." I rub my hand down my face. "I've been trying to reach my brother to see if he's had time to tinker some more. I'd like to have Rich's phone here so I can do some digging, but I can't reach Shane. He won't answer his damn phone."

"Maybe he's still out of the country," she suggests.

"It would help if he'd answer and tell me that."

Annika and Ivie return with a tray full of sandwiches and chips, soda, and water.

"I'm starving," Annika says, taking a sandwich and some chips for herself. "Eat up. There's more in the kitchen if you're still hungry."

"This is enough for an army," Nadia says and bites into a sandwich.

I try to call my brother again, but it goes straight to his voicemail.

"Son of a bitch," I mutter and then pin Ivie with a stare. She blinks and looks behind her.

"What?"

"I know you talk to my brother. Have you heard from him?"

"Shane?"

"Yes, Shane. Where the fuck is he?"

"I don't know." She shrugs and then says it again. "Honest, Carmine, I don't know. I haven't heard from him in a few days. He said he had some work to do and that he'd be in touch. Not to worry."

"Yeah. That sounds like him."

I bite into a turkey on rye and look around the room.

Nadia and I have been back in Denver for three days, and we haven't learned anything that we didn't already know when we arrived.

It's damn frustrating.

"If you hear from him, tell him to call me."

"I can do that."

"So, um, Annika," Nadia begins and smiles at her cousin, "Rafe asked about you the other day."

Annika doesn't even pause in the fast consumption of her chips. "Okay?"

"I told him to ask you, but he said you don't reply to his texts or calls."

"No." She slips another chip into her mouth. "I don't."

Nadia sighs and watches her cousin in exasperation. "Are you ever going to?"

Annika chews her bite, swallows, then looks at Nadia and says, "No."

"Why not?" Ivie asks. "He's a good guy, A."

"This is nobody's business," Annika replies and reaches for another bag of chips. "I'm just not going to, okay? I'm sorry, Carmine. I don't mean to insult you or anything."

"Rafe's an idiot," I reply happily. "I wouldn't reply, either."

"He's not an idiot," she says softly. "He's brilliant and kind and all of the good things that Rich wasn't."

She sets the unopened bag down.

"Then I'll ask again." Nadia's voice is gentle. "Why won't you answer him?"

I figure this must be what it's like to be a fly on the wall during a girls' night. I don't think I want to repeat the experience.

"Because I'm broken, and Rafe is way too good for me."

"That's a pile of bullshit," Nadia says simply. "You're not broken, and *no one* is too good for you, Annika Tarenkov. You're hurting, and you need time to heal. You'll get there."

Annika shrugs a shoulder and reaches for the laptop.

"Let's just get back to work and get this over with."

Time drags. Several hours and two sandwiches later, we're still at square one.

"I officially hate paper," I announce as I push the last folder aside. "And I know too much about all of these people's medical histories."

"Let's call it a day," Nadia suggests. "We can start again tomorrow with fresh eyes. Maybe we'll go to Rich's office."

"It's empty," Annika replies. "I went there to clean it out shortly after you left for Europe, but someone beat me to it. The only thing left was the desk."

"What?" I stare at her, dumbfounded. "Why didn't you say anything?"

"Because you were in France, on vacation. And, frankly, I didn't care. It was one less thing I had to deal with. Somebody did me a favor."

"He wouldn't have kept something incriminating there," Ivie says, shaking her head. "It wasn't secure, and he wasn't there all the time. If there's something that can help point to who's behind all of this, I think it'll be here. Rich was cocky. Arrogant. He felt safe here. Knew that no one would mess with him here."

"You're right," Annika agrees. "And I was *not* allowed to be in here. Especially when he was gone. If there's something to find, it's here."

"We need to stop for today," Nadia announces. "We're all moody and tired. We've been at it since sunrise. We need to get some rest and start again tomorrow, like I said."

I watch Nadia. She looks exhausted. We haven't stopped moving since France. There's been little time to rest and get over the jet lag.

She's not wrong. We do need to rest.

"You're right. We're probably missing something because we don't have our wits about us. Let's pick it up in the morning."

"Thank God." Annika closes the laptop. "I've tried every combination of words and numbers I can think of."

"If Shane would answer his phone, he could get into it without breaking a sweat. I'll keep trying him."

"I will, too," Ivie adds and reaches for her cell.

"It's settled then," Nadia says and stands to stretch. "We'll come back tomorrow."

"I NEEDED to get out of there," Nadia confesses when we pull into the driveway of our rental. "I love my cousin, you know I do, but she was irritating the shit out of me today."

"She's angry."

"She's being a brat," she counters. "And that's not like her. She won't talk to me. All she wants to do is brood and sulk, and it's irritating as fuck."

"Not everyone knows how to handle their emotions after a powerful loss like that."

"I know. And I'm sympathetic. She lost who she *thought* was her husband, the life she imagined they'd build together before he even died. And then he was just...gone. She couldn't confront him. She must have so many emotions going on, and I feel for her. But her attitude is shitty, and I needed a break."

"Fair enough." I park and lock my car, and we walk inside the house. It's the same one we used when we were here a few weeks ago. It's starting to feel like a home away from home.

I wonder if the owners would consider selling it? It would be convenient to have a piece of property here in the neutral city of Denver.

I'll have to make some inquiries.

"I'm taking a shower," Nadia announces, and already has her shirt over her head as she saunters down the hall to the master, her ass swaying in that way that never fails to kick me in the stomach with lust.

I want her.

I always want her.

I've fallen in love with her.

I follow after her and hear the water turn on in the shower. Deciding to leave her alone to wash off the frustration of the day, I light a few candles and then go to the kitchen to arrange some fruit, cheese, and crackers on a tray. It's not fancy, but it'll be a nice snack.

I set the platter next to the bed and turn to find Nadia standing in the doorway, towel-drying her hair.

She's naked and still damp from the shower. I can't wait to get my hands on her.

"Is that for me?"

"It seems that most of what I do these days is for you," I reply as I cross to her and cup her face in my hands. "Better?"

"Yeah, that felt good."

I kiss her lips tenderly. "Come, relax. Have a snack."

"I can think of something I'd like to snack on." Her lips curl up into a flirty smile, and she drops her hair towel to the floor, then reaches for my jeans.

"And what would that be?" The question is playful. "A card game, perhaps?"

"I'd kill you at poker."

"I've seen you play poker," I remind her.

"That was an act. I could have cleaned up on that table."

"Darling, you're just full of surprises."

She yanks my shirt over my head and tosses it to the floor, and then she's on me, raw need pouring from every pore of her body. We stumble to the bed, fall in a clumsy heap, and then it's all groping hands and laughter as we fumble our way to each other.

She's out of breath when I pin her beneath me, but her blue eyes are wild and locked on mine as I nudge her thighs apart with mine and drive home.

I gasp as she moans.

I *need* her the way I need air. I can't be gentle as pure desire fuels me, pushing and pulling, driving us both to the ultimate destination of eruption.

"Christ Jesus," she moans. Her back arches, and she clenches around me, then lets go.

I can't keep my hands off her breasts, my mouth away from her neck, and move up to her lips as I press on, still chasing the all-encompassing need to claim her. To show her how much I *need* her.

Finally, with my jaw clenched and my eyes shut, I fall over the edge and collapse on top of her, heaving and tingling.

I feel fingertips roaming over my spine and shift my face from the pillow to her neck.

"You're the best part of my life. Don't ever forget that."

Those fingertips still for just a moment but then begin moving again.

"I won't forget," she promises. "But you're going to have to move because I can't breathe."

I find the strength to roll to the side and smile over at her. "Sorry."

"It's okay. I'm mostly numb anyway." She giggles and reaches for a strawberry. "And I'm *so* hungry. Why am I so hungry?"

"You've been eating like a mouse since France."

"No, I haven't."

"Yes. You have."

She watches me and reaches for some cheese, then sits up to eat. "I've just had a lot on my mind, you know?"

"I do. And so do I. Don't worry, I'll keep an eye on you and make sure you eat."

"It's handy having you around."

"I'm glad you think so. Because I'd like to stick around for a long while. When all of this is done, I want you to move in with me."

She frowns. "Aren't I basically already moved in?"

"I want to make it official. I want to move all of your things to Seattle."

She swallows her cheese and watches me with those stunning eyes of hers. "To your house?"

"Yes. To my house. If you hate it, I'll sell it, and we'll buy something else."

She stands and reaches for her robe, wraps it around her, and turns back to me. "You'd sell your house for me if I didn't like it?"

Why do I feel like that's a trick question? "Of course, I would. I want to make a life with you, Nadia. I want you to live where you're comfortable and happy."

"In Seattle."

I see where this is going.

I tug on a pair of shorts and stand across the bed from her, my hands in my pockets.

"Yes, I'd like to live in Seattle. Is that a problem for you?"

"I don't know." She moves a piece of wet hair off her cheek. "It's not something I've considered before. Seattle is off-limits because our families—"

"Our families are fine. If you don't like Seattle, don't want to make a home there—"

"I didn't say that." She hurries around the bed and takes my hand in hers, then kisses my chin. "I'm over-thinking it. I like Seattle, Carmine. And I like your house. I mean, it could use a woman's touch here and there…"

Hope spreads through my belly.

"It could. You're right. Do you know of a woman who might want to add her touch?"

She smiles and tips her face to mine. "I just might. I'll put out some feelers."

"You're a sassy one."

"And you get to live with me. Lucky man."

Yes. Yes, I am a lucky man.

CHAPTER 18

~CARMINE~

I slept like the dead. I don't remember the last time I slept that hard.

I roll over and look at my watch.

9:30 a.m.

I sit up and scowl.

Nine-thirty? What in the actual fuck?

Nadia's already up. I don't know why she didn't wake me. It's completely uncharacteristic of me to sleep past seven.

I drag my hand down my face, then reach for my shorts. Jesus, jet lag is a motherfucker.

I pad into the kitchen and narrow my eyes. The whole house is still.

Where's Nadia?

Just as my phone rings in my hand, I notice the note on the counter.

C-

Ran out for donuts and coffee. You're so sleepy! Be back soon.

XO,

N

"Yeah?" I say without looking at the name on the display.

"You need to come up to Victor."

"Shane? What the fuck, Shane? I've been trying to reach you for days. Why don't you ever answer your goddamn phone?"

"I have a life, brother. But never mind that now. I need you to come up to my place to look at some stuff. Rocco's on his way to get you. Should be there any minute. I've been calling you for a few hours."

"I overslept." I sigh and scratch my scalp. "Christ, I haven't even had any coffee yet."

"I have plenty. Get your ass ready to go when Rocco gets there. Oh, and, Carmine, come without the girl."

"Why?"

"Just don't bring her. This is as confidential as it gets."

He ends the call, and I hurry back to the bedroom to get dressed and pull myself together. I usually trim the scruff on my face in the mornings, but there's no time for that today. I clean up a bit, comb my hair, and walk back out to the kitchen.

I look up to see Nadia coming through the door, juggling a box of her favorite donuts and a tray of coffees.

I rush over to help her, gratefully lift a coffee from the tray, and take a long sip.

"God bless you."

"Are you okay? You have sleep marks all over your face."

"I slept hard."

"Yeah, you did." Nadia lifts the lid of the box and sniffs the treats inside. "I bought too many, but I couldn't help myself."

"Thanks for going out to get this." I take her shoulders in my hands and kiss her. "I have to go."

"Huh? Where are we going?"

I kiss her forehead so I can stall and figure out a lie to use. I haven't had to lie to Nadia in months, and it leaves a sour taste in my mouth.

"I have to meet with my brothers. Some business that isn't tied to what we've been working on."

She nods and takes a bite out of a maple bar. "Okay. Are you sure you don't want me to go with you? We could go straight to Annika's from there."

There's a knock on the door.

"That's my brother. You know what? You take the car. I'll meet you there."

"Okay." She frowns, watching me. "Are you sure everything's okay?"

"As far as I know, everything's fine."

Rocco walks into the house and grins. "Mornin'."

"Hi, Rafe," Nadia says. "I didn't get enough coffee for you, but you're welcome to take a donut or two.

Actually, here. You might have just saved my life. I'll take two, and you guys take the rest. Now I won't eat them all myself."

"Nice. Thanks."

I take the box and kiss her again. "Thanks. I'll see you later."

"See you later," she says cheerfully as I close the door behind me and follow Rocco to his car.

"What the fuck is going on?" I demand when I climb into the rental.

"No idea," he says and stuffs half the donut into his mouth. After he swallows, he continues. "Got a call from Shane. Thirty minutes later, I was in the chopper headed here."

"Where's it parked?"

"Not far. We'll be at Shane's in an hour."

I feel sick after lying to Nadia.

We arrive at an airstrip where the chopper is waiting for us. Rocco and I climb in, buckle up, and he checks gauges and flips switches. When we have our headsets on, we take off.

The air over the high Rockies is choppy, so the ride is rough, but it doesn't take long before we land about a hundred yards from Shane's house on his property near Victor, Colorado.

As an old mining town in the mountains, Victor used to host more than a hundred thousand people. But now that most of the gold is gone, aside from the last few plots that large corporations own, the town has shrunk to just a couple of hundred people.

Just the way Shane likes it.

How he can live at ten thousand feet, in the middle of nowhere, I have no idea. The air is thin as hell, and it always takes me a day or two to get used to being up this high.

Rocco cuts the engine, and we get out of the helicopter and jog to the house where Shane's standing just outside his door, arms folded across his chest.

"Saved you a donut," Rocco says as he passes the box to Shane. "Your favorite."

"*One?*"

"Better than none," Rocco replies and shrugs as we follow our brother into the big farmhouse.

Shane's property is a fortress. Sitting on a few hundred acres, it's surrounded by state-of-the-art security with cameras and alarms. He has all kinds of toys, weapons, and other equipment that I probably don't want to know about, in addition to the helipad.

He leads us through a honey oak kitchen and the dining and living spaces, which all look completely normal. Fancy, but normal.

Then, he passes through a doorway and procedes down a long flight of stairs. When he flips on the lights, we're no longer in a simple farmhouse.

We're in a headquarters.

Machines beep and computers cover several desks. There are phones, screens, maps.

It's all very James Bond.

Or, Shane Martinelli.

"I got home a couple of days ago and was finally able to start digging into that slimeball, Richard," he begins with a donut in his mouth. "It was right there, in front of our faces the whole goddamn time."

"What was?" I demand.

"Let me start at the beginning." He flips on a screen, and it fills with a photo of Richard. "This asshole isn't Richard Donaldson at all. It's a cover. One that was well crafted, by the way. But it was thin. They didn't add layers, so I didn't have to dig far to discover that he's a phony. If Alex Tarenkov had done his job, it would have been harder to find. But, more on that in a minute."

He clicks a button, and data starts scrolling across the screen.

"Dimitri Lebedev." I turn to Shane in shock. "He's Russian?"

"Oh, he definitely is. But he was born in New York City in 1987. His parents were KGB spies in the seventies and early eighties and came to the US for asylum. The fucking government gave it to them in exchange for some information. You know, we were dealing with the Cold War at that time, and I'm sure they had plenty of secrets to share.

"So, our boy Dimitri was raised here in the US. Went to college at NYU. Smart kid, majored in PoliSci. Guess who his roommate was?"

Rocco and I stare at him. "Who?"

"Alexander Tarenkov."

Shane clicks some keys and some photos of the two men show up on the screen.

"Motherfucker," I mutter.

"So, these two were buddies in college. How Annika didn't know that, I have no idea. Because from what I've heard, Annika and Alex always got along well. Maybe Alex wasn't the type to bring his bestie from college home for the holidays. Maybe he knew if he brought Dimitri around his father, there would be trouble given that Dimitri's parents were KGB agents and all. But that's all speculation."

"We'll have to ask him," Rocco says.

"Wait a minute. If these are his parents"—I point to the couple on the screen—"who were the people at the wedding who claimed to be Rich's family?"

We all look at each other, and then Shane shrugs. "They were hired to act the part. This whole thing was a cover. But not for Dimitri."

"For Alex," Rocco finishes.

"Bingo. Whatever this jerk's into, it goes deep, and it's been going on for a long time. He had one arrest in college for dealing, but it was just some weed. Those records were buried. I assume thanks to his father."

"But the Tarenkovs don't deal," I say, shaking my head. "Nadia told me herself that drugs aren't their game."

"And I buy that," Shane says, continuing. "Igor has

always been adamant that their family isn't into the drug game. But that doesn't mean that *Alex* isn't."

"I need to ask Nadia—"

"Look, I know you're in love with her. Jesus, it's all over your face. But you need to tread carefully here," Shane interrupts, turning to me. "Because I have reason to believe that she's in on it with him."

No. Absolutely not. Everything in me wants to rail at him in anger, punch him in the fucking face for even *suggesting* that the woman I love is connected to this.

But I don't.

I wait.

Shane clicks more keys, and the photos on the monitor shift to ones of Nadia and Alex.

"These were taken just six months ago in Atlanta," Shane says.

The two of them are walking down the street together, laughing.

"The Tarenkovs are based in Atlanta," I remind him, but my gut is still in knots. Nadia hates her brother.

So why then is she in all of these photos with him, looking as close as two siblings can be?

"The point is, we don't *know*, Carmine. She could be playing you. She could be double-crossing you."

I remember what the goon in Cannes said: *"She'll just double-cross you, man. That's what she does."*

Fuck, has Nadia been playing me this whole time? I've been falling in love with her, and she's been playing me?

"Take me back." I march toward the steps, my heart pounding. I need to get to Nadia. I need to look her in the eyes when I confront her about this. "Right now, Rocco."

"We're all going," Shane says, shutting down the equipment in a rush and then running after us. "Goddamn it, slow down. I have to lock up."

"This place is a fucking fortress. No one even knows it's here."

"I know," he mutters before we all jog out to the waiting helicopter.

"I'M GOING IN ALONE." Rocco doesn't even pull into the driveway, he just pulls up to the curb. "I'll come to the office after I'm done confronting her."

"Are you sure she's here?" Shane asks.

"The car's still in the drive," I say with a nod. "She's here. I'll see you in a bit. Go see if you can find out where Alex is."

Rocco drives away as I walk up to the house. Jesus, am I completely blind when it comes to Nadia? I didn't go into this with the intention of falling in love with her. My guard was up, I was careful. Watchful.

I reach for the handle, but movement through the window in the door catches my eye, and I stop.

"Fuck me," I whisper. Nadia is sitting on the couch,

her back to me. And Alex, that son of a bitch, is pacing the living room, talking and gesturing with his hands.

Shane was right. The evidence is right here in front of me. Nadia didn't expect me back for hours, so Alex came over, and they're having a meeting in the house I'm paying for.

I pull my phone out of my pocket and call Shane.

"Yeah?"

"You need to come back here. Alex and Nadia are both here. I haven't gone in yet. I want backup. I know how badass she can be."

"On our way."

I shove my phone back into my pocket and decide to walk around the house to get a better view. We'll have to surprise them. Alex is weak and small, but Nadia is excellent at both hand-to-hand combat and with her weapon.

I ease my way around the opposite side of the room and peek my head around the window. Alex is standing in front of Nadia, his arms still flailing about.

And when he steps away, my blood turns to ice.

Nadia's hands are tied in front of her. Both eyes are blackened. Her shirt is ripped, probably from a struggle, and there's a gash in her shoulder with blood running down her chest.

The son of a bitch *hurt* her.

Nadia's eyes roam away from her brother and meet mine. They widen in surprise for a moment, and then she recovers. She watches Alex, who's still on a tirade, and then gives me a shake of the head.

It's barely noticeable, in case Alex sees her, but it's there.

She doesn't want me to come in.

Well, she's going to be very disappointed.

I hurry back around the house just in time to see my brothers hurrying up the driveway.

"He beat her up," I say quickly and bring them both up to speed. "She's not in on it, and he's going to kill her."

"No." Rocco takes out his sidearm and disengages the safety. "He isn't. How do you want to do this?"

"There are two entrances, aside from the garage." I point to the front door and then gesture to the side of the house. "Both are within his line of sight, so when we go in, we go in firing. But you have to be careful. Nadia's tied up on the couch."

"Rocco and I are going in on the side," Shane says, cool as a cucumber as he thinks it through. "Carmine, you go in through the front door as if you're just coming home and don't know what's going on. Play stupid with him for a bit. We need to catch him off guard."

"And if he just draws a weapon and shoots me?"

Shane smiles. "Duck."

"That's not helpful." I tap my piece at my ankle and the one at my back. "He's yelling. I'd say he's telling her everything he's done."

"Alex *would* brag," Rocco says. "He'll want to tell her everything before he kills her."

"I'm using that to my advantage," I say and walk to the door. "Get in position. I'm going in."

Without another word, I open the door.

"Hey, babe, I'm home! I hope there are still some donuts left. I'm starving. The gym was pretty empty today, so—"

I come up short when Alex points a gun in my face.

"Hey, hey, hey, what's going on? Nadia?"

"Hello, *darling*," Alex says with a sneer. "Go sit with her. This works out well. I can kill you both at the same time."

CHAPTER 19

*N*o. All I can think is *no.*

Alex is going to kill me.

And now, he's going to kill Carmine, too.

"Let Carmine go," I say through throbbing lips. "This is between you and me."

Instead of answering, Alex slaps me and then lowers his face to mine and sneers. "Papa didn't teach you to keep your cunt mouth shut, so I'm going to do it. Don't you fucking talk unless I tell you to."

"Why'd you do it?" Carmine asks calmly as he sits next to me. "Why'd you enlist Rich and go about this whole dramatic game?"

"Game?" Alex turns on Carmine but doesn't hit him. No, he's too much of a pussy to hit a man stronger than he is. "This isn't a game. This is brilliant. I was just telling little sis here all about it, but I'll explain it to you, too. She'll just have to hear it twice. But you don't mind, do you, sis?"

I shake my head no. From the corner of my eye, I see Carmine slip his phone out of his pocket. He taps on the screen, but I can't see what he's doing.

Hell, *he* can't see what he's doing.

"Papa is too set in his ways," Alex begins. "He's weak. He thinks we should respect the old ways of doing things. And because of that shortsightedness, he's missing out on a lot of money. I'm not willing to do that."

"You're not rich enough?" Carmine asks.

"Fuck, no. Who's *rich enough*? There's no such thing, you dumbass. Drugs. Drugs are where it's at. And when you have a new brew, all the better."

"That *new brew* you have kills people," Carmine says. "That doesn't make for repeat customers."

"That's not what we were selling." Alex laughs. "That was just to get people out of our way. The stuff we sell is the best high you can have. It's better than coke, better than meth or anything else. People will be *begging* me for it. They'll pay anything at all for it."

"What is it?" Carmine asks.

"It's a synthetic. You don't have to sniff it or shoot it. You pop the pill, and in twenty minutes, you're on the best ride of your life. I call it Hades."

"How original," Carmine says calmly. "So, you went to some of Sergi's people in New York, and they turned you down."

"Weak assholes," he says with the shake of his head. "They didn't want to do anything unless they ran it by Mick first. And I couldn't allow that."

"Why not?"

"Because this is *my* fucking operation," Alex yells and drives his finger into his chest. "Mine. Not theirs. And if they want to try to bring anyone higher up in, they get dead."

"So, what about Richard? Or should I say, *Dimitri?*"

What? Who in the hell is Dimitri?

Alex's smile falls, and he wipes his mouth with the back of his hand before smiling again, but I can tell he's nervous now.

"I figured you'd find out about that sooner or later," Alex says. "It was so pitifully easy. With his background, he was just itching to get into something on the down-low. Something big. It was his idea to marry into the family. I thought he should marry Nadia." He turns to me, and I want to throw up. "But he had a thing for Annika. He said Annika was weaker and would be easier to fool. And I hate to admit it, but he was right. She fell for the whole sappy I-love-you act—hook, line, and sinker. I mean, he actually got her to *marry* him! Women are so stupid. So easily manipulated. They're fucking worthless."

He turns to me and raises his hand, but Carmine stops him. He's up in a flash and has Alex's wrist in his fist.

"If you touch her one more time, I'll rip your

goddamn arm off."

Alex shoves away like a pouty child. "Don't touch me. Don't fucking touch me."

He reaches for his gun, but it's gone.

"Looking for this?" Carmine holds it up, and Alex's face goes white.

Oh my God. We're going to live through this.

We're going to live through this.

Carmine throws the gun across the room and turns to me.

"Don't—" I begin, but it's too late. Alex hits Carmine over the head with the tray that was on the coffee table. Carmine turns and backhands Alex, but then, to both of our surprise, Alex retaliates.

Carmine takes as many hits as he dishes out. I rush across the room and retrieve the gun, my hands still tied with the twine Alex brought with him. Still, I'm able to point it down at my brother, who's now bleeding from the nose.

"Freeze."

Suddenly, Rafe and Shane run into the room, their weapons drawn, and Alex sags against the hardwood in defeat.

"Fuck," he says and then coughs and looks at me. "I will kill you. It may not be today, but it's going to happen. My men should have done it in France, but they were too weak. I knew I should have done it myself. And I will. Every minute of your life, you'd better sleep with one eye open and watch your back."

I look at Carmine. "Did you record everything he said earlier?"

He grabs his phone and nods. "It's on here. But I learned everything from Shane. That's where I was this morning."

I look over at Shane as Alex starts to moan and whine. "Do you have all of the evidence my father will need to prove that my brother was behind everything?"

"I do," Shane says with a solemn nod.

With the gun still in my hand, I look down at my brother, and I squeeze the trigger, killing him instantly.

"Call the cleanup team." I drop the gun and let Carmine fold me into his arms. I ache all over from the beating Alex gave me, and my heart hurts, too.

"Shh." Carmine rocks me back and forth. "I'm so sorry, baby."

"He was an ass. A complete ass. But he was also my brother. And there was a time that I loved him."

"I know." He kisses the top of my head. "Come on. Let's get you cleaned up."

"We've got this," Shane says, but before we can leave the room, he kisses my cheek. "You did the right thing."

"Sometimes, the right thing really sucks."

"I know."

"Don't worry about this," Rafe says kindly.

"I have to call my father. There's different protocol here."

"I know," Rafe says. "Don't worry."

Carmine leads me to the bathroom off the master,

closes the door, and I fall into his arms, sobbing like I never have before.

"I'm a monster." I pull back, just out of his grasp. "Jesus, Carmine, I'm a monster. I killed my brother."

Without a word, he takes my shoulders and turns me to look into the mirror, pressed close behind me.

"Look at yourself."

My eyes are swollen and blackened. My lips are puffy and split. I have a cut on my shoulder from the kitchen knife.

"He knocked on the door about thirty minutes after you left," I begin and swallow hard. "Of course, I let him in. Turned my back. And he started in on me. He had a baseball bat. I couldn't react. Couldn't defend myself."

"He was a coward."

"He told me that he was behind all of the killings. Said that he was going to kill me, then Papa. That he'd be the boss. Said he'd turn our family into a drug lord empire—exactly what Papa doesn't want."

"And he was going to continue hunting you, would try to end your life, Nadia," he reminds me. "That wasn't an empty threat. If I hadn't arrived when I did, you'd probably be dead now. Can you look us both in the eyes and say that what you did was wrong?"

"No." I shake my head slowly. "I don't think it was wrong. Because he would have killed you, too, and I couldn't live—"

I turn back into his arms. "I couldn't live with

myself if he hurt you, Carmine. I love you so much, I can't bear the thought. Oh my God, what would I do without you?"

He tips my chin up with his finger. "Do you mind saying that again?"

"What would I do without you?" I sniff, more tears falling at the thought of Carmine being gone.

"Not that part, baby."

"I love you, Carmine. I don't know how it happened or when. We went from being enemies to *this.* But I do. I love you so much it hurts. I really thought you'd come into this house and find me dead. That alone almost broke me. But then when I thought that he might kill *you,* as well, I just… You are the best part of my life."

"I think that's my line." His lips touch the side of mine, ever so gently so he doesn't hurt me. "I love you, too. With all of my heart and soul. You are meant to be with me. I feel that in my heart."

"I do, too." I snuggle into him for just a moment. "We'd better get me cleaned up so I can face my father. I don't know what he'll do."

"He'll love you," he says simply. "And he'll grieve."

"Yeah." I nod as Carmine reaches for a washrag. "We'll both do that."

SIX OF US sit in my father's living room in Atlanta. Carmine and his brothers flew me here this afternoon, and their father, Carlo, met us.

We didn't meet at an office.

We came to Igor Tarenkov's home.

"Your mother is lying down after taking a sedative," Papa says as he reaches for me. His eyes are shadowed and sad, but he touches me with tenderness. "How do you feel, little one?"

"A bit sore. It's not as bad as it was in Seattle when I got—" I stop talking at my father's furious look and swallow hard. "Oh, I guess I forgot to tell you about that."

"I suggest you tell me now."

I look over at Carmine, who's sitting next to his father. All four men are imposing. Carmine nods. "It's time, sweetheart."

So, I take a deep breath and tell them all about getting attacked in Seattle, and how Carmine and his people helped me get well.

"But that wasn't the first time."

I tell him everything, going back to when I was jumped in Atlanta, and my hair was cut.

"It seems your brother has been terrorizing you for a long time," Papa says quietly. "I'm sorry. I'm sorry that I never saw it. I should have known."

"He was good at covering his tracks," I remind him. "Papa, I understand if you don't want to see me again. If this is goodbye—"

"What kind of nonsense is this?"

"I killed your son." I bury my face in my hands and

weep. "I murdered my brother in cold blood, and I would do it again. What kind of daughter does that make me? What kind of boss would I make?"

"No one asked for my opinion," Carlo says, catching my attention, "but I'm going to give it anyway. You would make an excellent leader, my dear. Because you did what you had to do to keep the rest of your family and those you care about safe. Your brother was the bad seed. And I hope I'm not speaking out of turn when I say we all saw that."

"You're not," Papa says. "I will grieve for the son I had and the man I needed him to be. But the punishment fit the crime here, Nadia. Don't torture yourself. You were defending yourself. And me."

Relief floods me. "Thank you."

"I'm sorry for the way this ended," Carlo says to my father. "If there is anything my family can do for you, we are always at your disposal."

"Thank you, old friend," Papa says. "And likewise."

"We still haven't figured out who killed Elena's parents," Rafe points out. "That goes back farther than Alex."

"That's something we'll have to keep digging into," Shane agrees. "We'll find them."

"I have something to say," Carmine says. "Mr. Tarenkov, I'd like to ask for your permission to marry your daughter."

My eyes fly to Carmine's in surprise.

Our fathers share a smile.

"Well, it's about damn time, my boy," Papa says. "Carlo and I have been throwing you at each other for years."

"I thought they'd never come to their senses," Carlo says with a laugh. "A couple of stubborn children we have here, Igor."

"Wait. You *wanted* us to marry?" Carmine asks.

"Of course. Why do you think we've allowed you to spend so much time together?" My father winks at me. *Winks!* I don't think I've ever seen him wink a day in his life.

"How do you like that?" Shane says with a laugh. "Pop's a matchmaker."

The brothers both laugh as Carmine crosses to me with humor in his chocolate brown eyes.

He lowers to one knee.

"Will you marry me, Nadia, and be the best part of my life until I'm no longer on this Earth?"

"Let me think about it." I grin as he digs into his pocket and comes out with a rock the size of a baby's fist. "Geez, Carmine. Did you have to get something so fancy?"

"Yes." He slips it onto my finger and then kisses my knuckles. "I'm going to give you everything you've ever dreamed of."

"I believe you." He kisses me carefully.

"Is that a yes?"

"That's a hell yes."

EPILOGUE

~IVIE~

*I*t's been a long-ass day at the clinic. Annika took off for home about an hour ago, but I decided to stay and clean up a bit. Annika just hasn't been herself over the past month or so, not since her husband died.

I'm worried about her.

So, if I can stay late at work, make sure everything is perfect for her here and take some of the burdens off her, I'll gladly do it.

Annika is my best friend. She's the only person in the world who knows my deepest secrets. And I'll do whatever it takes to help her.

I hear the bell on the front door and hurry out to tell whoever it is that we're closed.

But when I get there, I stop cold.

"Hello, Ivie." He flips the lock on the door, and I dial

Annika's number and leave my phone on the desk so she can hear everything. I hope with all my might that she answers. "Or should I say, *Laryssa?*"

I shake my head. "I'm sorry, I don't know a Laryssa. I'm Ivie. And we're closed for the day. But if you'd like to make an appointment, I can help you with that."

"You know, I thought for a long time that your father was an imbecile. Stupid. He didn't cover his tracks well."

I just raise my chin, determined not to let him see my fear.

"But you're different. You covered your tracks *very* well. And I know that you couldn't have done that alone. Which tells me that your father isn't as stupid as I thought."

"I don't know what you could possibly want from me. I'm just living my life."

"And a nice life it is," he says. "Good for you, Laryssa. I couldn't make your father pay for his sins when he was alive—and we both know that those sins were many. But now I've found you."

I shake my head as he walks around the counter.

"Now, don't do something silly like try to get away. You're coming with me. And you're going to pay for the sins of your father."

He jabs a syringe into my arm, and I immediately feel…heavy.

"There, now. Come along, Laryssa. We have plenty of work to do."

. . .

DON'T MISS HEADHUNTER, the next book in the With Me In Seattle MAFIA series! You can get it here: www.kristenprobyauthor.com/headhunter

AND HERE IS a sneak peek at Headhunter:

HEADHUNTER

A WITH ME IN SEATTLE MAFIA NOVEL

PROLOGUE

~IVIE~

"I'm not doing this for you anymore." I glare at my father and raise my chin, trying to appear way more confident than I feel.

My stomach pitches when he slowly turns to glare at me with cold, blue eyes. The same eyes that look back at me in the mirror.

But I'm nothing like the man who sired me. And I never will be.

Without another word, he turns back to the task at hand, making an egg sandwich. Our apartment is small and in a dirty little neighborhood in the Bronx. He says it helps us blend in, that no one will pay us any mind here.

In reality, he spends money as quickly as it lands in his pocket, and this is all he can afford.

I turn sixteen this summer, and he's already made it

clear that I'll be quitting school and taking a full-time job.

What I want doesn't matter. It never has with this man.

"Did you hear me?" I demand.

"I hear nothing important." His voice is calm, thick with that Bulgarian accent that I hate so much.

"I'm serious. I'm not doing your bidding anymore. If I get caught, I'll go to *jail.*"

"You are too young for jail."

"No." I shake my head and plant my hands on my hips. "I'm not too young. They'll send me to juvie. Either way, I'll be locked up, and I'm not doing that for you. This is ridiculous. Why can't you be a normal father instead of gambling and selling fake jewelry? Why don't you just get a real job so we can live a normal life?"

Without a look, he spins and backhands me, sending me sprawling on the floor. My cheek sings in pain, and I see stars as he leans over so close that his nose nudges mine.

"You are my *property,*" he growls. "You are nothing but a female. And you'll do exactly as I say, *when* I say. If you try to defy me again, I'll sell you to the many men who have already asked for your body."

I gasp and stare up at him in utter shock and revulsion. "You *wouldn't.*"

"Yes." He stands and straightens his crisp, white shirt. "I would. Do not test me again, Laryssa."

The knock on the door is sharp, startling us both.

"I know you're in there, Pavlov," a man yells through the door, and all the blood drains from my father's face.

"How?" he whispers and then turns to me. "Hide me, daughter."

I shake my head, only enraging him further. He raises a hand, but before he can hit me for a second time, someone busts the door open, and three men walk inside.

"Did you think you could steal from us and get away with it?" The biggest one reaches for my father and pushes him against the wall.

This is it. This is my chance.

I scurry into my little bedroom and grab the bag I always keep packed—always ready to run if the opportunity arises.

I won't get another chance like this.

"No, I wouldn't steal from you. I just had to earn the money to repay you."

Another man punches him in the face as I slip out the front door and make a run for it.

My heart hammers in my chest. I can't hear the street noises through the rush of blood in my head and over my loud, panting breaths.

I have exactly four hundred and thirty-two dollars, some clothing, and my mother's wedding ring.

And a new freedom.

Because I'm *never* going back to live with a man who makes me do the things my father does.

I'll die first.

CHAPTER 1

~SHANE~

"Take the shot."

The voice is calm in my ear, coming from several thousand miles away in a secure office at the White House.

I'm lying on my stomach on a rooftop, my sights trained on the target, but people keep walking in front of him.

"Not clear," I whisper and swear when the target walks into another room.

"It's taken three weeks for you to find him," the president reminds me. "Take him out. *Now.*"

Yeah, yeah. I don't need her to remind me how long I searched for this asshole. And as soon as he moves a little to the left…

I squeeze the trigger, and less than a second later, the target falls.

"Mission accomplished," I say and move quickly to the stairwell that leads to a waiting car below.

In less than three minutes, I'm safely away from the scene and headed to the airport.

"Good work," she says into my ear. "Now, get yourself home. The plane's waiting for you."

"Thank you, Madame President."

I nod to the driver, my partner for this operation, and he steps on the gas to get us to the airfield quicker.

Suddenly, the front window explodes, a bullet hitting the driver squarely in the forehead, killing him instantly.

"Miller's down," I say with a calm I don't feel as I reach over to take the wheel. I maneuver him out of the seat and manage to step on the gas, winding my way through the foreign city.

If I'm caught, I'll also be killed.

And I'm not ready to die today.

Only one car is following me, and it doesn't take me long to lose them.

"Your transport has been compromised," I hear in my ear. "The crew was killed. I need you to disappear for a couple of days. Lay low and await further instructions."

"Abandoning me in a foreign country wasn't part of the deal."

"We're not abandoning you," the president replies. "We'll get you out."

"See that you do."

"WE EXPECTED you home a few days ago," my brother, Carmine, says as I walk into his office at our family's base of operations in Seattle, Washington. Rocco, my other brother, stares out the window but turns to look at me as I move farther in.

"Yeah, well, I got hung up."

I won't mention that I spent two nights curled up under a box, waiting for the US government to get me out of enemy territory after I assassinated one of the bad guys.

My brothers aren't allowed to know any of that.

It's better this way. The less they know, the less likely they could be killed for having the knowledge.

"Have I missed anything important?"

"Wedding plans," Rocco volunteers and then smiles at our brother sweetly. "I mean, it was a rough few days there, deciding between lilacs and freesia. And then there was the matter of the cake flavors."

My gaze bounces between Rocco—who's clearly getting a huge kick out of razzing our big brother—and Carmine, whose mouth firms into a hard line.

"He's the groom," I say simply and cross to the small kitchenette to see what kind of food we have stashed away in the fridge.

I'm fucking starving.

"I never pegged Nadia as the type to get all swept up in the fancy wedding deal," Rocco says thoughtfully.

"She's a woman," Carmine reminds him. "And big weddings are the mafia's way. You know that."

"So, which was it? Lilacs or freesia?" I ask as I return to the desk with a half-eaten sub sandwich and a bag of nacho chips.

"Both," Carmine says with a shrug. "She couldn't decide, so we went with both."

"As one does," Rocco says with a wink.

The door bursts open, and the bride-to-be herself hurries inside, her eyes wide with an emotion I rarely see on my brother's fiancée.

Fear.

"Carmine," she says as she hurries over. "I have Annika on the phone. She needs our help."

"Put her on speaker," I say, and we all lean in to hear what Nadia's cousin has to say.

"Okay, they can all hear you," Nadia says as she plants her hands on the desk. "Tell them *exactly* what you just told me."

"It's Ivie," Annika says, immediately getting my full and undivided attention. "She's been taken."

"Taken by *who*?" I ask, keeping my voice calm but feeling my blood erupt through my veins with a surge of new adrenaline.

"I don't know," she says and sniffs. "I got a call from her, but I was about to get in the shower, so I let it go to voicemail."

She sniffs again, frustrating me.

Just fucking *tell me*.

254

"I remembered it the next morning, *this* morning, so I listened to it. Oh my God, you guys. She's been taken. She was trying to get me to pick up, to listen, and help her. And I failed her horribly. I need you. Is Shane there?"

"I'm here."

"Thank God. Please, we need your help."

We all look at Rocco, who's already pulling his phone out of his pocket.

"The plane will be ready when we get to the airport."

"I THOUGHT Annika was going to tell me that this was all connected to Rich," Nadia says, shaking her head as the plane lands in Denver. "That there was more information or that someone else was dead. *Something.* I didn't expect her to tell me that Ivie had been taken."

I swallow hard, fear a very real and icy demon settling in my stomach.

I don't fear much. But Ivie and I have become friends over the past several months, and if my life weren't well and truly a shitshow, I'd take it much, much further with her.

If anyone touches a hair on her gorgeous head, I'll fucking skin them alive.

"Rich's organization fell," Carmine reminds his fiancée.

"We don't know that now," Nadia says, shaking her head. "Maybe this is tied to that. Maybe someone thinks they can get something out of Annika, or punish her by taking Ivie."

"We don't know what's going on," I remind everyone. "Let's get to Annika's place and figure things out."

My mind is racing. I haven't slept in seventy-two hours, and aside from the stale sandwich, I haven't eaten.

And I don't give a shit.

I need to find Ivie. Make sure she's safe and whole.

Annika's house is an hour from the airfield.

"You should sleep," Nadia says to me, her voice soothing. "I can see that whatever job you were on took a toll. You need rest if you're going to help Ivie."

"I'm fine."

"You're not fine," she counters, and I *barely* stop myself from rolling my eyes at her.

Nadia is a fierce woman. I don't need her to kick my ass over an eye roll.

"I'm *fine*," I repeat and narrow my eyes at her.

"What is it with the Martinelli brothers and being so fucking stubborn?" she asks as she turns back in her seat and scowls out the windshield.

"It's just part of our charm," Carmine says, but Nadia shakes her head.

"No, actually, it's not charming. It's dumb. He's going to hurt himself if he keeps overworking like that."

As if I have a choice. I can't exactly tell her that I sleep when the fucking *president* says I can.

So, I just grunt and watch Denver whiz by outside the window. The few hours it took to get here is, unfortunately, valuable time wasted. Time that I could have spent trying to find Ivie.

Jesus, where is she? What are they doing to her? And *who the fuck* are *they*?

"Almost there," Rocco mutters and sends me a sympathetic smile.

I know my brothers are aware of the massive crush I have on Ivie. I've never had a *crush* on anyone in my fucking life. But I saw her once, and that was all it took.

I know that Rocco and Carmine don't understand my attraction. That's because she's a little awkward and has a classic, girl-next-door look about her that I find absolutely hot as hell. She's not the type that would usually turn my head, and my siblings know it.

In the past, that may have been true.

But Ivie attracts me in every damn way. She's funny and sweet. *So* damn sweet. We've spent a little time on the phone, talking. I'm not much of a talker, but it comes so easily with Ivie.

How my brothers *don't* see the amazing woman she is, is beyond me.

I know that a relationship—hell, a *future*—with Ivie is out of the question for someone like me. My job consumes my life, and what's left over belongs to my family. Between the government and the mafia, I've killed more than any one man should. My time doesn't belong to me.

But if things were different, if I were free to be my own man, I would scoop Ivie up and make her mine in a heartbeat.

"She looks worse than the day she found out that Rich was a lying asshole," Nadia says as we pull into Annika's drive and see the woman standing in the doorway, waiting for us.

Her eyes are red-rimmed from crying, her nose chapped from wiping it too much. And when Nadia hurries to her and engulfs Annika in a hug, the other woman falls apart once more.

"Let's go inside," Carmine says, urging the women into the house and to the living room.

When Annika's seated and wiping her wet eyes, Carmine speaks again.

"Now, tell us again *exactly* what happened."

"Okay." Annika takes a long, deep breath and then tells us again about seeing the call from Ivie, but how she let it go to voicemail because she was getting into the shower and how she didn't remember about the call until this morning.

"So I finally listened to the message, and my blood ran cold."

"Play it," I say, sitting next to her as she pulls it up on her phone, taps the screen, and it starts to play.

"I'm sorry, I don't know a Laryssa. I'm Ivie. And we're

closed for the day. But if you'd like to make an appointment, I can help you with that."

"You know, I thought for a long time that your father was an imbecile. Stupid. He didn't cover his tracks well. But you're different. You covered your tracks very well. And I know that you couldn't have done that alone. Which tells me that your father isn't as stupid as I thought."

"I don't know what you could possibly want from me. I'm just living my life."

"And a nice life it is," the man says. "Good for you, Laryssa. I couldn't make your father pay for his sins when he was alive—and we both know that those sins were many. But now I've found you. Now, don't do something silly like try to get away. You're coming with me. And you're going to pay for the sins of your father."

There's a pause.

"There, now. Come along, Laryssa. We have plenty of work to do."

"After that, it's dead air for a couple of minutes, and then it ends," Annika says, locking her phone.

"Do you recognize his voice?" I ask her.

"No. I didn't recognize his face, either."

My head whips up. "You saw his face?"

"Yes, we have security cameras at the spa, of course. I looked at the footage, but I don't know who he is."

"I can find out," I reply. "I'll need to see it."

Annika nods, but Carmine shakes his head.

"He kept calling her Laryssa. That's not her name. Could she be a victim of mistaken identity?"

"No," Annika says softly and then stands to pace the room. "I can't believe I'm about to tell you this, but she's in danger, and you *have* to know."

My hands curl into fists.

"Know what?" I demand.

"Ivie's real name is Laryssa Pavlov. Her father was a Bulgarian asshole, but she escaped him when she was young. Made a new life for herself—one she could be proud of."

I can't believe what I'm hearing. After all the hours Ivie and I spent talking, she never told me any of this.

"So, this guy really is trying to punish her for her father's sins," Rocco says, blowing out a breath.

My brother's eyes haven't left Annika. It's no surprise he doesn't give me a hard time about Ivie. He, too, longs for someone he can't have.

It's a shitty situation to be in.

"What was her father's name?"

"Ivan. Ivan Pavlov," Annika says. "I can't tell you much about her past. She told me the story in confidence, but this definitely has something to do with her father."

"Get me that footage so I can find this motherfucker and get Ivie home where she belongs."

"Of course," Annika says, reaching for her laptop.

"I need to transfer this file to my system," I inform her, already tapping the keys on her computer. "I can find out who he is by running the face through some software and a database I have."

My hands fly over the keyboard, and then I reach into my bag for my laptop and get to work again, fingers flying.

When the screen simply says *Searching...* for what feels like a fucking year, I want to punch my hand through a wall.

But, finally, an image and bio appear on the screen.

"Boris Nicolov, fifty-eight. Bulgarian. Last known address is in New York. Looks like I'm going to the east coast."

I stand, and Rocco joins me. "Maybe you should do some more digging before you head off on a wild goose chase."

I push my brother against the wall and get up in his face.

"Get the fuck out of my way."

"Hey." His hands come up in surrender. "I'm not *in* your way. I'm just, you know, trying to be the voice of reason."

"Either you'll help me, or I'll do this without you."

"You know we'll help," Nadia says.

"I'll inform the Sergi family that we'll be on their turf for this," Carmine adds, referencing another mafia family. No one just shows up on another family's turf. You always let them know in advance.

"I didn't even think of that," I mutter and rub my hand down my face. "Thanks. Let's do this."

"Keep me posted," Annika says as she hurries

behind us to the door. "I guess I could have shown you all of this while you were still in Seattle."

"It's better in person," I reply and then reach back to squeeze her hand. "And this way, we're closer to New York than we were a few hours ago."

She offers me a watery smile, and Nadia, Carmine, and I all hurry back to the car.

Rocco hangs back to say something to Annika that has her tearing up again, then he jumps in the car with us, and we're off to the airfield.

"What did you say to her?" I ask quietly.

"It doesn't matter."

DON'T FORGET to get your copy here: https://www.kristenprobyauthor.com/headhunter

NEWSLETTER SIGN UP

I hope you enjoyed reading this story as much as I enjoyed writing it! For upcoming book news, be sure to join my newsletter! I promise I will only send you news-filled mail, and none of the spam. You can sign up here:

https://mailchi.mp/kristenproby.com/ newsletter-sign-up

ALSO BY KRISTEN PROBY:

Other Books by Kristen Proby

The With Me In Seattle Series

Come Away With Me
Under The Mistletoe With Me
Fight With Me
Play With Me
Rock With Me
Safe With Me
Tied With Me
Breathe With Me
Forever With Me
Stay With Me
Indulge With Me
Love With Me
Dance With Me

ALSO BY KRISTEN PROBY:

Dream With Me
You Belong With Me
Imagine With Me
Shine With Me
Escape With Me

Check out the full series here: https://www.
kristenprobyauthor.com/with-me-in-seattle

The Big Sky Universe

Love Under the Big Sky
Loving Cara
Seducing Lauren
Falling for Jillian
Saving Grace

The Big Sky
Charming Hannah
Kissing Jenna
Waiting for Willa
Soaring With Fallon

Big Sky Royal
Enchanting Sebastian
Enticing Liam
Taunting Callum

Heroes of Big Sky

Honor
Courage

Check out the full Big Sky universe here: https://
www.kristenprobyauthor.com/under-the-big-sky

Bayou Magic
Shadows
Spells

Check out the full series here: https://www.
kristenprobyauthor.com/bayou-magic

The Romancing Manhattan Series

All the Way
All it Takes
After All

Check out the full series here: https://www.
kristenprobyauthor.com/romancing-manhattan

The Boudreaux Series

Easy Love
Easy Charm
Easy Melody
Easy Kisses
Easy Magic

Easy Fortune

Easy Nights

Check out the full series here: https://www.
kristenprobyauthor.com/boudreaux

The Fusion Series

Listen to Me

Close to You

Blush for Me

The Beauty of Us

Savor You

Check out the full series here: https://www.
kristenprobyauthor.com/fusion

From 1001 Dark Nights

Easy With You

Easy For Keeps

No Reservations

Tempting Brooke

Wonder With Me

Shine With Me

Kristen Proby's Crossover Collection

Soaring with Fallon, A Big Sky Novel

Wicked Force: A Wicked Horse Vegas/Big Sky Novella
By Sawyer Bennett

All Stars Fall: A Seaside Pictures/Big Sky Novella
By Rachel Van Dyken

Hold On: A Play On/Big Sky Novella
By Samantha Young

Worth Fighting For: A Warrior Fight Club/Big Sky
Novella
By Laura Kaye

Crazy Imperfect Love: A Dirty Dicks/Big Sky Novella
By K.L. Grayson

Nothing Without You: A Forever Yours/Big Sky
Novella
By Monica Murphy

Check out the entire Crossover Collection here:
https://www.kristenprobyauthor.com/kristen-proby-crossover-collection

ABOUT THE AUTHOR

Kristen Proby has published close to forty titles, many of which have hit the USA Today, New York Times and Wall Street Journal Bestsellers lists. She continues to self publish, best known for her With Me In Seattle and Boudreaux series, as well as several others.

Kristen and her husband, John, make their home in her hometown of Whitefish, Montana with their two cats and dog.

facebook.com/booksbykristenproby
instagram.com/kristenproby
bookbub.com/profile/kristen-proby
goodreads.com/kristenproby

Made in the USA
Middletown, DE
19 September 2021

48654130R00165